Requiem In Red

A Cressa Carraway Musical Mystery

Kaye George

Barking Rain Press

This is a work of fiction. Names, characters, places, and events described herein are products of the author's imagination or are used fictitiously. Any resemblance to actual events, locations, organizations, or persons, living or dead, is entirely coincidental.

Requiem in Red: A Cressa Carraway Musical Mystery
Cressa Carraway Musical Mysteries, Book 2

Copyright © 2016 Kaye George (www.KayeGeorge.com)

All rights reserved. No part of this book may be used or reproduced in any manner whatsoever without written permission, except in the case of brief quotations embodied in critical articles and reviews.

"Hymn of Promise" by Natalie Sleeth © 1986 Hope Publishing Co., Carol Stream, IL, 60188. All rights reserved. Used by permission. Reprinted under license #77756

Edited by: Rachel Roddy (www.facebook.com/rcwriter)
    Ti Locke (www.urban-gals-go-feral.blogspot.com)

Proofread by Colleen Romaniuk (www.RomaniukCol.wordpress.com)

Cover artwork by Stephanie Bibb Flint (www.sbibb.wordpress.com)

Barking Rain Press
PO Box 822674
Vancouver, WA 98682 USA
www.BarkingRainPress.org

ISBN Trade Paperback: 1-941295-43-6
ISBN eBook: 1-941295-44-4
Library of Congress Control Number: 2015952741

First Edition: April 2016
Printed in the United States of America

9 7 8 1 9 4 1 2 9 5 5 4 3 4

DEDICATION

To the good people of the former
Hopkins United Methodist Church
and to the Minnetonka Orchestra.
I spent many happy hours in both places.

Also Available from Kaye George

Einc Kleine Murder: *A Cressa Carraway Musical Mystery,* Book 1

Choke: *Imogene Duckworthy Mysteries,* Book 1
Smoke: *Imogene Duckworthy Mysteries,* Book 2
Broke: *Imogene Duckworthy Mysteries,* Book 3

Death in the Time of Ice: *A People of the Wind Mystery,* Book 1

As Janet Cantrell

Fat Cat at Large: *Fat Cat Mysteries,* Book 1
Fat Cat Spreads Out: *Fat Cat Mysteries,* Book 2

Coming Soon from Kaye George

Death on the Trek: *A People of the Wind Mystery,* Book 2

Coming Soon from Janet Cantrell

Fat Cat Takes the Cake: *Fat Cat Mysteries,* Book 3

www.KayeGeorge.com

Playlist

TITLE	COMPOSER
Orchestral Suite #2 in B minor	Johann Sebastian Bach
Rondo alla Turka	Wolfgang Amadeus Mozart
Trout Quintet	Franz Schubert
Prayer from Hansel and Gretel	Englebert Humperdinck
Für Elise	Ludwig van Beethoven
Hymn of Promise	Natalie Sleeth
Trouble in River City (from *The Music Man*)	Meredith Wilson
Seventy-Six Trombones (from *The Music Man*)	Meredith Wilson
Jesu, Joy of Man's Desiring	Johann Sebastian Bach
Lord of the Dance	Methodist hymn (261)
This Is My Song	Methodist hymn (437)
There Is a Balm in Gilead	Methodist hymn (375)
Christ, Whose Glory Fills the Skies	Presbyterian hymn (47)
I to the Hills Will Lift My Eyes	Presbyterian hymn (377)
Jesus Christ is Risen Today	Presbyterian hymn (204)
The Lord Ascendeth Up on High	Presbyterian hymn (212)

For links to these songs on YouTube, visit:
www.BarkingRainPress.org

Chapter 1

Prélude: A piece of music designed to be played as an introduction... to another composition, such as a fugue or suite (Fr.)

October

I glanced in the tiny, cracked mirror that hung just inside the stage curtain. My straps weren't showing. My plain brown hair lay reasonably compliant, and there was no food in my teeth. Examining myself in mirrors was unusual behavior for me. But then again, this wasn't a usual night.

The voice onstage droned on and on. "...our own. She's studied hard and achieved stellar grades in the music graduate program here at DePaul University. This piece is her first chance to conduct a full symphony playing her own original composition in front of a live audience."

The announcer thundered the last phrase. "And so I ask you to welcome, Cressa Carraway!"

My introduction had ended. The polite, mildly-interested applause had died out. It was time.

I squared my shoulders and stepped into the footlights, squinting a bit at the harsh glare. This was my debut. The moment I'd waited years for. Just past the curtain, I paused and gave the audience a slight bow, then continued to the podium. Thank God I didn't trip climbing onto it. I hoped they wouldn't be able to see my heart thumping through my new black dress.

I gave another nod, this one to the concert mistress, who rose and cued the oboe to give the pure 440 concert A. After the orchestra was tuned and the first violin player was reseated, I opened the score to the first page and picked up the baton.

Fifty-four eyes bored into mine, waiting.

Deep breath. Another one.

The baton shook slightly in my hand, but not too bad.

I was about to conduct the symphony I'd written for my master's thesis in music composition. I'd named it "Affirmation" and dedicated it to Gram—my grandmother—who had encouraged me to pursue the career I wanted in classical music. Gram was dead, but she would live through my music. I drew one more breath, let a nervous smile spread across my face, and started conducting.

Time receded and the music took over. There was nothing but the music, and it was happening. *My* music was happening!

Half an hour later, the three-movement piece was done.

I cut off the final chord with a flick of my wrist. My hands no longer shook. The baton was steady. I gave the orchestra a grin to show my appreciation and turned to face the audience.

In the split second after I turned, paralyzing fear spun my mind in whirls. What if they didn't applaud? What if they hated it? Would anyone boo? That half-second took an eternity. My public face, I was sure, looked like a Halloween house mask—a stiff grimace below widened, frightened eyes.

Then the sound of clapping started. I relaxed my face muscles into something more human. Three people in the first row jumped to their feet and many followed suit. One person yelled, "Brava," then another.

I bowed twice, then stretched my hand out to include the musicians in the ovation. What a great feeling!

It was over. I had premiered. I had debuted. I had done it. Cressa Carraway was a symphony orchestra conductor.

Maddy Streete studied the thin young woman who had been holding her wine glass for at least fifteen minutes without taking a sip. The woman hadn't had a chance to get a plate of goodies either. The long table held chocolate-dipped strawberries, grapes, petit fours, and other delicacies Maddy hadn't even explored yet.

Poor thing, thought Maddy.

Maddy watched Ms. Carraway, who wasn't imposing, like some conductors. She was unremarkable looking, medium height, medium-brown hair. But she was as poised as she had been at the podium while she accepted congratulations on her success in the auditorium tonight. Maddy made her way across the reception room in the lower level of the concert hall. As she reached the conductor, two of the people around her left, leaving Maddy a clear field.

"Hi, I'm Maddy, Madison Streete." Maddy stuck out her hand and they shook. Cressa's hand was cold, but her grip was sure.

"I'm sorry for my cold hands. Madison Streete?" Cressa looked confused.

"I know." Maddy laughed. "I'm not sure what possessed me to marry a man named Streete. I sound like I should be driven on in downtown Chicago when

I use my full name. My name has an extra 'e' on the end, so I'm not exactly the street."

Cressa laughed. "I think it's a great name, Madison. I was just trying to place you. You're the one I wrote to about the job in Minnesota."

"Please call me Maddy. Yes, and I'd like to talk about the job. Can we go somewhere to talk after this?"

Cressa looked apprehensive. "Sure, I'd love to."

She doesn't know if she's going to be accepted or turned down, Maddy thought. Maddy smiled to set her at ease. "I like your style. Can you come to Minnetonka to audition?"

Maddy was glad she'd made the trip to Chicago to hear the concert. She had a feeling Cressa was just the person she needed.

Chapter 2

Da capo: From the beginning (Ital.)

Early December

I gazed out the plane window. I had felt trapped during the flight to Minneapolis, sitting in the window seat and unable to get out, but now I was glad I had the seat. The diamond-bright lights of the city glittered below me. It made me nervous that I couldn't quite recall what Maddy looked like.

From what I could remember, she seemed only two or three years older than me. I also remembered the sound of her voice, and the Minnesota accent with its luscious long O's. But her hair, had it been dark blond or light brown? We had only talked a few minutes that night. Maddy was meeting me at the airport, but what if I didn't recognize her? That would be a great start to my audition. The night I met her, I'd been so nervous, even after the performance, that the whole evening was a blur.

My parting with Daryl had gotten this whole trip off on a bad foot. I could tell he didn't want me to even try out for this job. It would be fine with him if I stayed at DePaul the rest of my life, stuck in a job I disliked. Would I be the same way if he had a chance to move somewhere to further his career? I hoped not.

I rubbed my little finger, wondering if the altitude was making it ache. It had been broken in the past and reacted to the strangest things.

The announcement came to put our seat backs in the upright position, a distance of one inch from the reclining position. I pushed the tray table up and turned the fasteners. One was broken. The tray hung drunkenly, but stayed out of the way. *Here goes nothing*, I thought.

Maddy was a bit worried. She shifted her weight from one foot to the other and picked at the corner of her cardboard sign, watching the passengers coming into the baggage claim area. It was so cold, with people opening the outside doors every two minutes, that she left her coat and hat on.

She waved a sign that said "Cressa Carraway" and hoped she'd recognize her charge. They had met only briefly two months ago and Maddy wasn't sure she'd know her again. After all, she was so ordinary looking.

But that wasn't her main worry.

Her cell phone chirped from deep within her coat pocket, and she tucked the sign under her chin to dig it out. It was her brother, Barry, her main worry in life. Maddy sighed, then pushed the answer button.

"Maddy, I don't know what to do. I can't, I can't…"

"Barry, slow down." He was getting bad again. This was discouraging. "Where are you?"

"I'm home, Sis. But I'm all alone. How could he? He's gone. How could he do this?" He started sobbing. "We were so…He just doesn't…How can I…"

"Barry, stop!" she shouted.

Heads whirled in her direction and she lowered her voice.

"I need to come over, to see you," she continued, hunching down and turning her back on the staring crowd. "But I can't come over right now. Later. Sometime tonight, I promise. Wait for me. I'll be there right after the interview. Just sit tight and—"

"Hi. Maddy? I'm Cressa." She stuck her hand out for Maddy to shake. "You are Maddy Streete, right?"

Maddy punched the button to end the call and straightened up. In a flurry of confusion, Maddy dropped her sign, stuck her cell phone into her purse, and took Cressa's hand.

"It's me, underneath my winter coat and hat," Maddy said. After Cressa picked up the sign, Maddy pulled her gloves out of her pocket, then grabbed one of Cressa's two bags and led the way out of the shelter of the airport terminal and into the icy December blast.

"Brrr," said Cressa giving an exaggerated shiver. She put on her own hat and gloves and tugged her thin scarf tighter around her neck.

"I don't think Minneapolis is any colder than Chicago, is it?" Maddy asked.

The wind whipped mini-tornadoes of dry snow around their ankles. The lights of the parking lot caught the glint of a few swirling flakes in the gloomy afternoon. "Well…" Cressa hesitated. She looked doubtful as she glanced at Maddy, who was leaning into the weather. Maddy could feel her cheeks starting to glow, a vibrant, alive feeling. She turned to Cressa in the dim, watery sunlight.

"I'm probably crazy," Maddy said, "but I love this weather. This is what living in Minnesota is all about."

"Maybe our weather in Chicago isn't different, but our attitude sure is," said Cressa. "The Chicagoans I know hate winter. Do people in Minnesota love it?"

It was Maddy's turn to laugh. "I think most of us do. We're all a little nuts."

Her car was parked close in, they weren't in the icy wind for long. After they stowed Cressa's luggage in the back and climbed into the Explorer, Maddy started the engine and cranked the heat all the way up.

"We got this cold wave day before yesterday," she said, backing out of her space. "I guess this is your welcoming committee. This way you'll know what you're getting yourself into if you accept the job."

She steered around the corners of the labyrinthine garage, searching for the exit.

"First I have to get an offer, right?"

"Well, yes. You have a good chance, though."

"I'm excited about this," Cressa said. "And nervous, too. Do I conduct first or interview first?"

"This afternoon you'll be interviewed by a panel of four people, and that's scary enough. Tonight, the chamber ensemble meets and you'll conduct them."

"Are the others here, too?"

"Yes, all six candidates for the job will interview this morning and will conduct tonight. We—the chamber ensemble and the board—will vote this evening. We might pick our new conductor tonight, but we'll have to wait for the next board meeting to make it official."

She glanced at Cressa to see what effect her words had, but Cressa just nodded. Maddy was glad to see she looked confident. Maddy's reputation was on the line. After she'd heard Cressa conduct in October, she'd recommended her to be the one to help the local chamber group start on their expansion plans. The board had decided to grow the small ensemble group into a symphony orchestra and needed just the right person to get it off the ground. They wanted someone young and energetic, but a musician who knows his stuff. Or her stuff. That's what the board stipulated. Maddy had assured them she had found the right person. The proof would be today.

I approached the long, plastic table and Maddy slipped into the interview room behind me. The room held the table and some folding chairs, plus an old wooden desk in the corner beside two tall filing cabinets.

A small rotund man motioned me to the head of the table, the most conspicuous, uncomfortable spot, of course. He introduced himself and the others. Due to my nerves, I missed his name, but caught that he was a banker-philanthropist who was funding the group as it grew. The interview panel consisted of Maddy, who was the concertmistress—lead violin—of the small musical group, the round banker, another violinist, and a man named Roger Hirt, who seemed to be a local musician of some sort.

I reeled off my credentials and told them I'd studied conducting with the Conductor Emeritus of the Chicago Symphony while I was studying for my master's degree. I saw one smile—Maddy's—and two nods when I said that last bit. After a few easy-to-answer musical questions, I began to relax and let my spine rest against the back of the padded folding chair.

"It's obvious from your answers that you would know what to do with a baton," said Roger Hirt. That made me feel even better.

"What do you like about chamber music?" asked Heidi, the other violinist, a tall blond woman. "Wouldn't you rather conduct a large orchestra?"

She wasn't smiling, I guessed this wasn't a joke. The bad cop, I thought, with the tough questions. I wouldn't fly here to audition if I wanted to conduct nothing but symphonies. I felt my chest flutter and tighten up.

"I grew up playing chamber music." My voice sounded calm, I thought. I couldn't hear a quiver and hoped they couldn't either. "I love conducting an orchestra and the challenge of performing a full symphony, but the intimacy of a chamber group is more personal. To me, a chamber ensemble is the gentle relative of a big, bombastic symphony orchestra."

Did that sound like horseshit? I saw the group nod. So far, so good. The tightness loosened and the flutter went down a notch. Maybe I'd better ask some questions, too. "What are the future plans for this group?" I said. "Will it always be a chamber ensemble?"

Roger Hirt answered. "We'd like to perform as a chamber group for another year or so. Certainly we'll finish this season as a chamber ensemble. We want to expand and someday become a full-fledged orchestra. Gradually, not right away."

"Sounds like an exciting job prospect." And it was. The scope of the undertaking was exhilarating. I fished a paper Maddy had mailed to me out of my purse. "I noticed in this schedule that you've already had one concert. Who conducted that one?"

"I did," answered Roger. "I led the fall rehearsals and the first concert in November. After we hire a permanent conductor, I'm willing to remain on the board in an advisory capacity."

I thought I'd like that, as the man was not bad looking at all, from what I could see of him from across the table. He was older than my twenty-four years—those lines in his face might put him at late thirties. His blue eyes sparked when they met mine and I could feel the heat, whether he intended it or not.

A tweet made everyone look for their cell phones. It was Maddy's.

"Sorry," she said, embarrassed, and hurried out the door.

Maddy walked down the central hallway of the community center, far enough that the board couldn't hear her through the closed door.

This time it was her younger brother, Frank, who lived in Apple Valley. Not too far away, but not as close to Barry as she did. Frank was about a half hour away, if the traffic was good. Thus, it fell to her most often to look after their older brother, Barry, who was in Hopkins, where Maddy's family lived.

"Maddy." His voice, usually smooth and calm, broke on her name. "I'm really worried about Barry this time. I just got a weird call from him. Something is bothering him, but he won't tell me what it is."

"I got a call, too, and I told him I'd go over later. I'm in the middle of some interviews and can't talk for long, but what did he say?" She and Frank should be used to worrying about Barry by now, but she would never get used to it.

"He was angry at someone—Woody, he called him. Said something about, 'Woody can't do this to me,' but I couldn't calm him down enough to figure out what the problem is."

"I'll go over there as soon as I can, Frank. I gotta run now."

"Should I ask how you think it went?" asked Cressa, fastening her seat belt. Her fingers were a bit unsteady. Maddy saw Cressa's adrenaline surge was lasting longer than the interview. That happened to her when she played solos, too.

"You did fine, Cressa," Maddy said. And she did think Cressa had a good shot. Especially since the panel interview had gone well. Cressa didn't have as many formal credentials as some of the other interviewees, but she did have Maddy's personal recommendation. Maddy knew she herself carried weight with the chamber orchestra, since she was one of the founders and was first-chair violin in the group.

If Cressa had turned out to be unsuitable, it would be a reflection on her, she was relieved to see that her protégée had made a favorable impression. At least one thing was going right today.

"Good," said Cressa. "The more I hear about this job, the more I want it."

"You don't mind moving from Chicago?" Maddy knew she would never be able to move away from her family.

Cressa paused, then answered. "Not really."

She didn't sound convincing. Maddy wondered what that was about. Maybe Cressa did have doubts about relocating.

Maddy stopped at Barry's after dropping Cressa off at her hotel, but he didn't answer her three doorbell rings and many knocks. Her heart rose nearly to her throat with the last fist beat on the unyielding wood.

Barry's disappearance last July ran through Maddy's mind. When he'd surfaced after a month, she had needed to monitor his bipolar medicine daily for a couple of weeks until he was stable again. It was like having another child, one harder to deal with than her two young ones.

He'd been a troubled teenager and young man, but she and Frank thought he seemed more at peace lately. He'd announced, just a few months ago, that he was gay and he'd settled down. Until now.

Before she drove away, she left a message for him from her cell phone.

Barry called back five minutes later, just as she was pulling into traffic on the main road. He pretty much repeated what he'd said to Frank, ranting and not making much sense.

"Maddy, he doesn't understand," he sobbed. "I thought we had…I thought we would—"

"Barry!" she shouted. "I'm driving. I shouldn't even be talking on the phone."

He was quiet for only a second. "You said you'd be here."

"I was just there. You didn't answer the door."

"Come back! Please hurry. I'll be right here."

"I can't do it right now. After the tryouts, later tonight."

"All right. I'll be here."

"And answer the door?"

"Yeah, and answer the door, too," he said, with a whine in his voice.

She had to leave it at that. She hoped there wouldn't be a repeat disappearance. Holidays had always been a tough time for Barry. He just wasn't able to be jolly on command.

In the evening, all the candidates met at the local high school. Maddy drove me again, in her SUV, complete with two car seats in the back.

Roger told us that each candidate would lead the group for ten minutes. We sat on metal folding chairs in a dim hallway outside the high school orchestra room and were called in one by one. The room was sound-proofed; I couldn't hear how my fellow contenders were doing.

I was the last to audition. I sat in the hallway, practicing deep breathing and wiping my sweaty palms on my slacks, telling myself to calm down. I closed my eyes and tried to slow my heartbeat, but it didn't work any better than it ever did. At last, my name was called and my heartbeat spiraled upward. I entered the room and crossed to the podium. I tripped mounting it. *Great start, Cressa,* I told myself.

Maddy, sitting first chair, just to my left, gave me an encouraging look.

"Hi," I began. The group smiled up at me. Deep breath. I looked down at the music on the heavy black stand in front of me, unseen and unknown until this moment. It was the Bach Orchestral Suite #2 in B minor. I let my breath out slowly in relief. All the conductor candidates were conducting the same piece. And this was one I knew well. I felt my body tension go down a notch.

"It looks like you're working on the Bach?"

They nodded. No one pointed out what a stupid question that was.

"Okay, anybody want to tune?"

When several cellos and a viola nodded, I looked around and flipped the switch on the electronic tuner I spied on a table near my stand. Everyone listened to the 440 A for about three seconds, did some perfunctory tuning, then became quiet.

I grinned at the faces turned upward toward me, most of them wearing bland, non-committal smiles below expectant eyebrows, and took one last deep breath. If I didn't quit this, I'd hyperventilate and pass out. I hadn't been this nervous for my conducting debut in October, but I had known what to expect then. I didn't know this group.

"First movement first, okay?"

I raised the baton, the violins and violas tucked their instruments under their chins, the cellos raised their bows, and the one flute licked her lips. My baton quivered. Maddy sat with her back straight, bow poised on the string. Heidi, the tall blond from the meeting, sat on the second stand, right behind Maddy. She didn't look hostile at all here.

We were ready. Then I had a second thought and hesitated. These were amateurs, and this piece could cause some problems if the musicians weren't familiar with it.

I put down the baton and pointed out the pitfall of the Overture, which has a rhythm that is never played as it's written.

"Just want to make sure that all of you know to double-dot here. Make the long notes longer and the short notes shorter than written," I said. "This movement is hard to keep crisp if you're not concentrating all the way through."

Maddy gave me another encouraging look and a nod.

Then I raised the baton again, my hand nice and steady now, and led them through a page and a half of that movement, stopping a couple of times when the rhythm was getting sloppy, in order to re-emphasize the timing.

I remembered to cue the flute, trying for an easy, but exacting, conducting style. I mimicked favorite conductors I'd worked with, which was turning into my own style as I went through graduate school. This group would help me refine it further. If I got the job. The ensemble was easy to work with, and made up of good musicians. I could hear that already. The clunkers and stumbles were few and far between.

"Okay, guys," I said when they stopped. I glanced at my wrist watch. "This is a monstrous-long piece—eight movements, and I only have ten minutes, so we'll have to pick and choose, we can't do it all. I'd like to start the second movement. It's a little tricky too, because although there are four beats in every measure, it sounds as if the first beat always comes in the middle of the measure, on the third beat. So count carefully and watch my downbeat or you'll start thinking that the third beat is really the first."

Maddy felt that Cressa's conducting was clear and easy to follow. They stopped only a few times, once when the violas missed an entrance.

After a page of the second movement, Cressa stopped them with a quick cutoff motion, then put her hands down and said, "Let's do the last movement, just because it's so much fun."

It was one of Maddy's favorites, too. She often used it as a wedding recessional with her string quartet because of its rollicking joy.

In the middle of a passage, the first chair cello player and official timekeeper looked at his wristwatch, waved his bow around above his head, and announced that Cressa's time was up.

At this, Cressa cut them off, thanked them, and said she'd had a great time. Maddy was sure it wasn't something Cressa would want to do every day, in spite of her words. Cressa put down her baton, got off the podium without falling, and left the practice hall.

Maddy drove Cressa back to the hotel, promising to let her know the decision as soon as she could, then returned. The group that had done the interview in the afternoon had put away their instruments and Maddy walked into an ongoing discussion. They were agreeing that Cressa Carraway was their first choice. One point in her favor was her smile. Some of the candidates had been so serious that they came across as stern. Two of the six didn't seem to know the piece very well, which surprised Maddy since it was a standard piece for chamber orchestras. After their next official board meeting, they would notify all the candidates and make the offer to Cressa. Maddy wished she could let Cressa know right away.

Barry didn't answer the door when Maddy went by on her way home. She pounded for a good five minutes, finally banging her head on the door a few times in frustration.

So much for his promise to be there.

She didn't know if she could go through this again.

Chapter 3

Deciso: Decided, energetic, with decision (Ital.)

Early January

On a Monday in early January I got the phone call telling me the Hopkins Chamber Orchestra wanted me—me, Cressa Caraway—for their conductor. My interview must have gone even better than I thought, which was pretty darn good.

The first thing I did, after letting out a scream and dancing around my living room, was call Neek, my own personal seeress from the apartment across the hall. Neek's aging hippy parents had named her Unity Unique, but she preferred Neek, for obvious reasons.

"Hey, I've got big news," I said.

"Hold on a sec. I have to stop my zen-pilates video." After a pause she came back. "Okay, what's up?"

I told her of my offer to conduct the Hopkins Chamber Ensemble. "I'm so excited! I really, really wanted this job." I sat on the couch, bouncing just a bit.

"Ah, that's what it means."

"I'm afraid to ask, but, that's what *what* means?" Neek sees portents in, well, objects. Sometimes odd, random objects.

"That weird rock I found today. It was perfectly striped brown and gray. Like it was painted. I knew that meant a new job for somebody, just didn't know it was you. But wait, does that mean you're moving to Minnesota?"

"Yep."

"What about Daryl?"

"Well…" That was a problem, actually. "I haven't called him yet."

"What will he say?"

"I'm not sure. I hope he'll be happy for me." I felt my knee jiggling up and down. A sign I was nervous about telling him, even if I wouldn't admit it.

"Yeah, but?"

"But I really don't know. I'm afraid he'll think it's a whim. He knows I haven't liked my job here from the beginning, but he keeps saying I'll learn to like it. He can't understand why I even interviewed at Hopkins." I put my hand on my knee to keep it still.

"Learn to like it? A job you don't like? And why should you?" "Exactly! Why should I tolerate a job when I can actually like one? I know I'll love this one." My knee started up again.

"My rock says it's a good thing."

"It's settled then. I'm going."

Daryl—we had been seeing each other for a year and a half. Last fall, we both got jobs teaching at DePaul University, Daryl in art, me in music, so we could be together. Daryl was a visual artist, specializing in painting and sculpture, and he was doing well with his showings in and around Chicago. He loved his teaching job, and only partly because the college studio provided him with space and materials for his private work. In fact, his private endeavors were actively encouraged since the more of a reputation he acquired, the better it reflected on the school.

I liked my job okay most days, but wasn't just lovin' it the way Daryl was lovin' his. Not having time to work on my own compositions frustrated me, and I really do like to write music, more than about anything. A lot of my hours, and too much energy, were taken up teaching two music theory classes, grading papers and tests. I didn't even have time to practice piano because I was busy preparing lessons for my private pupils. I hadn't done much private music teaching before, no years of experience to tell me what each kid should be playing at his or her level of expertise, and I started from scratch with each student. I sometimes felt I was thrashing around at DePaul, waiting for something better to happen.

This conducting position, though, this would be less structured, I would probably have more time to compose and to just play when I felt like it. What's more, maybe this was the something better I was waiting for.

Although, with the part-time salary being offered, it was clear I would have to do something to supplement my income. That something would most likely involve playing piano or organ somewhere. I didn't think that would be too hard to manage. Dance studios and churches are always looking for keyboard players.

After I hung up from my acceptance call to Maddy Streete, I had a moment of uncertainty. Could I make this job work? Would they like me? More importantly, would they keep me? There were a lot of details to be ironed out—probably more than I had thought of yet.

My parents—and my Gram—didn't raise a coward, though. And, as I never forgot for long, Minnesota was where my mother and father had met their deaths. I felt a pull to the place because of that. Even though their deaths had been explained to me many times, the story always seemed incomplete. Maybe I would go and see where their car had gone off the icy road after their gig. That'd been New Year's Day, thirteen years ago, when I was eleven years old.

I called Daryl and asked him to meet me for lunch at the off-campus cafeteria near his building. When he arrived, twenty minutes late, I was waiting at a table with a salad from the salad bar.

"Had a student that needed some help with perspective," he said, shedding his coat and scarf. His brilliant blue eyes shone in his freckled face as he leaned to greet me with a quick kiss. He pulled his knit cap off his unruly copper curls, then noticed my full plate. "You're starting without me?"

"I was hungry. Go get something and I'll wait."

He gave me a cool look and went to stand in the line for the buffet. The line was much longer now than when I'd gone through it, at our agreed time.

After he came back with a plate of roast beef and mashed potatoes, much more appropriate for this winter weather than my salad, I had to admit. I said I had something to tell him.

"Uh-oh. That doesn't sound good."

"No, no, it's good. I have a new job." I loaded my fork and didn't meet his eyes.

"Really? With DePaul? Doing something different?" He loaded his, too, with mashed potatoes, and stuffed them into his mouth.

"Well, no, it's in Minnesota." I met his eyes.

"Minnesota?" He dropped his fork onto the plate with a clatter and gulped down the mouthful of potato. "You live here."

"Well, yes. The job is in Minnesota."

"It's that thing you flew there for, isn't it? I knew you shouldn't have gone. You're moving?"

"I'm moving to Minnesota."

"You said that. Is it a real job? Are you quitting your job here? How can you do that? How long will you be there?"

"Yes, I'll give notice tomorrow."

"When will you be back here?"

"It's a brand new group," I enthused, trying to infect him. "They want to grow from a small chamber ensemble into a full-fledged community orchestra."

"And?"

"And that will take time. They trust me. They think I'm the person who can do that."

"Six months? A year?" He stabbed a piece of beef and chomped it viciously.

"Probably longer." Probably several years, I thought.

"But you don't have to stay there the whole time. You can just get them started, then come back here. I bet the university would take you back."

He wasn't making this easy.

"Look, for that matter, *you* could find a job in Minnesota. Your credentials are excellent and every school needs an art teacher."

"I *have* a job. You do, too."

I *had* a job. One I detested. A job I was quitting. "Yes, I do." I felt my voice getting shrill. "I'm moving to Minnesota for it."

"Let's talk about this later." He spoke through clenched teeth. "I gotta run. See you tonight?"

He left his unfinished meal on his plate and put on his coat, rushing into the cold. No good-bye kiss. As I watched him go, I crossed a lightly penciled line through Daryl's name in my mind. If he wasn't going to go along with my dream, I'd go it alone.

I was too busy to see him that night. Instead, I booked an apartment in Hopkins, a moving van, and an airline flight. A few days later, I kissed dear Daryl good-bye at the airport and flew off to start my new life. Despite my air of confidence, I had a pit in my stomach.

What on earth was I doing?

Chapter 4

Leggero: Light, airy (Ital.)

Joshua crept into the Presbyterian church, a place he'd never been before. It was late afternoon. He had seen the two secretaries leave a half an hour ago. The earth was dry. It hadn't snowed for over a week in Hopkins, and the little bit of cover that had been on the ground was gone. The weather was cold, but that didn't bother Joshua much. Internally, deep inside, he felt warm and drowsy from the Big H. He thought he might find a place in the Presbyterian church to crash for a while.

It was Tuesday, Joshua thought. Last night he had been discovered in the high school locker room and kicked out. The janitor found him going through the open lockers looking for something to steal. He'd gotten away with a couple of good watches and a bottle of cheap bourbon from a football player's locker, though. He had exchanged the watches for pot and smack.

He found the church kitchen in the basement and grabbed a handful of cookies from a paper plate on the counter. He was trying to pat the plastic wrap back in place over the cookies when a tall older man poked his head through the door and started yelling at him. Joshua shoved past him and stumbled out, hoping he was retaining some dignity, like he wasn't a vagrant.

In truth, the Reverend Willard Linger recoiled at the strong odors wafting from the young man who brushed by him. If he had to guess, he would assume a medley of the heady smell of liquor, the sour smell of an unwashed body, and another sweeter smell he couldn't identify. With the culture of today, though, Willard gathered it must be some sort of drug.

Willard followed him up the stairs to make sure the young vagrant left the building, then turned the deadbolt. Usually, the front doors were already locked by that time of night, but Willard had stayed late to do some more reading for his sermon next Sunday. He always found it hard to get motivated right after the Advent and Christmas season. Epiphany in January was something of a letdown. Then nothing much happened, liturgically, until the spring and Lent, which led up to Easter.

In fact, Willard was having a hard time getting motivated at all this year. He had fallen into a crushing depression that had lasted throughout the Christmas season. Even now, after the season was over—the one hardest on lonely people—his spirits wouldn't lift. He sighed as he turned from the double entry doors, now locked. He ambled down the hallway to his office and sat dully staring at his computer monitor.

Nothing seemed to matter much since Wilma's death two years ago. He'd never gotten over the fact, and maybe never would, that her uterus had killed her. For all the years they'd tried to have children, the damn thing never worked. Then, in the end, it had killed her with its evil cancer.

"Damn you, God," Willard whispered, afraid that if he shouted, God would hear him too well. His faith was profoundly shaken by her senseless death, and, increasingly, his world was fragmenting around him, shattering into incoherent, sharp bits. He tried to ignore a thought that, in recent weeks, was gaining the upper hand against his resistance—the thought that Wilma's death was his punishment. He twisted in his swivel chair. His bible lay on the corner of his desk. He opened it randomly and Psalm 61 looked up at him:

> Hear my cry, O God;
> listen to my prayer.
> From the end of the earth I call to you,
> when my heart is faint.
> Lead me to the rock that is higher than I;
> for you are my refuge,
> a strong tower against the enemy.

The verse failed to lift his spirits in the way he knew it should. He knew this was his failing, not God's. He knew the high places were the most sacred. He knew the answer for him had something to do with that.

Willard closed the book, put on his coat, and left for his empty home, neglecting to turn off the lights or check any of the several side and back entrances to the building.

Joshua, now shivering in the bushes that lined the Presbyterian church parking lot, saw the tall, balding old man drive away. He walked around to the rear of the church, pulled the door open, and smiled. He paused to rub his cold hands together, then went back down the stairs, finished the cookies, and found his way to a pretty parlor with upholstered furniture. The heat had been left on and it was nice and warm. He flung the stupid, small pillows off the soft couch onto the carpet and soon fell asleep. Maybe he could forget for a few hours.

I awoke Wednesday morning in my new apartment on Shady Oak Lane in Hopkins, my new hometown, a close-in suburb of Minneapolis. I loved the name of the street. Maybe it was why I'd chosen this apartment building. A storm had threatened yesterday, but the bad weather had held off as I had scurried around signing things for the lease and doing a bit of exploring. This morning, though, the clouds loomed more ominously.

In spite of the gloomy weather, I bounced around my new place, humming Mozart's happy *Rondo alla Turka*. My new place smelled clean. The paint was fresh, the carpeting was new. I stepped onto my balcony. Across the street was a lovely little duck pond surrounded by oak trees. I came back inside and closed the balcony doors. The place was empty, stark—my furniture was arriving tomorrow, on Thursday. I had slept on the floor and was somewhat stiff. I took a brisk walk around the pond across the street and then felt rarin' to go.

The Chamber Ensemble Board was meeting at ten o'clock and Maddy had said I needed to attend. On the way there, I found a bakery a couple of streets away and grabbed breakfast. My car was supposed to arrive on the truck with my furniture, so I was renting a small gray Toyota until it came. That should be tomorrow, the movers had told me.

I kept turning on the windshield washers when I tried to put it into gear. After the third time, I burst out laughing. Everything was fine today. Then I remembered I'd forgotten to call Daryl yesterday. I had promised him I'd call when I was settled in. I would, for sure, call him tonight.

I got to the meeting early, but Roger Hirt, who I now knew would be my boss, was already there. His hand was warm as he shook mine and reintroduced himself. I remembered him, though. It had only been a month. Plus, with a face and body like that, who wouldn't? Or rather, what female wouldn't?

"Hi, Cressa," he said. "It's so good to see you again."

Likewise, you'd better believe it.

"Have a seat." He waved me to a folding chair around the same table where my interview had been conducted, in the community center.

"Are you still conducting the chamber group?"

"Not since our last concert. I've been too busy with my other orchestra, so we took a break."

"You have another orchestra?"

"It's the one I've had for a few years. I conduct the Minnetonka Symphony," he continued. "I don't know if you knew that, but it's why I conducted here until a permanent replacement could be found."

"Is that a professional group?"

"No, it's a community orchestra, but quite a good one. I'm also principal trombone in the Minnesota Orchestra."

"Wow, I'm impressed. You're busy. And principal with Minnesota—that's a top-notch professional group."

"But where would we be without the amateurs? I'll tell you. We'd be minus about a hundred American orchestras."

"That's for sure." Okay, enough about showing off Roger's knowledge and abilities. "I know I'm going to enjoy this job." Was that gushing? I felt like it was.

We chatted for a few more minutes about whether or not it would snow. The rest of the board arrived soon after, and I listened as they discussed fund raising. Maddy, my new friend, was also there. Roger took an armful of music from Maddy and gave it to me to go through.

I was introduced to everyone at the end of the meeting, rather than the beginning. I thought that was a little odd. The reception seemed a few degrees below warm, but not exactly chilly. They all smiled politely, but I could sense a wariness toward me, now that I was officially the newcomer. As the meeting broke up, I tried to catch Roger, then Maddy, but they both rushed off. All and all, a little disappointing. These Minnesotans weren't that easy to get to know.

So I took my pile of scores and went back to my apartment to delve through them. My enthusiasm had dampened, and I felt a little deflated. I tried to get back my morning mood by going over the scores. Soon, I was humming passages, determined to recapture some of my eagerness.

I *was* going to love this job! I'd show Daryl. He thought I never should have come here. Thoughts of Daryl strayed to thoughts of Roger.

No, I told myself, you have Daryl. Or you did. You don't need Roger right now. That would be too complicated.

Maddy left the Chamber Board meeting in a hurry, feeling awful about not stopping to talk to their new conductor. But she knew Barry would get impatient or might even leave if she were late for their lunch date. He had such strange ideas about punctuality. He was obsessed with being on time and got anxious if other people were late. Sometimes it was hard for her to believe they were siblings. Maddy had gotten all the "late" genes and Barry had all the "early" ones.

Barry had called her the night before and apologized for standing her up in December. The family hadn't seen him the rest of the month, even for Christmas. But last night he'd offered to buy her lunch if she met him right after the board meeting. She'd hated to run out on Cressa like that—Cressa looked like she wanted to talk—but Barry was a bigger concern for her right now.

She pulled into the parking lot of the Wendy's on Wayzata Boulevard, relieved to see Barry's Jeep in the parking lot.

"Hey, Sis." He greeted her with a kiss on the cheek when she found him at a booth in the back.

"You're in a good mood," she remarked, hoping this was a good sign.

"Yeah, better than I've been lately."

They went to the counter and ordered. Barry got a hamburger and fries, and Maddy ordered a baked potato, which she loaded from the salad bar. Then they returned to their booth. Barry liked to sit in corners where he could check out the whole room. There was a bit of paranoia in him, along with his other conditions.

"Well, here's why I asked you to lunch," he started between bites. "I want to apologize. I'm sorry I put you and Frank through so much last month."

"I'm just sorry you missed Christmas. We would have liked to have you there with us, Barry," she said with a tender smile. She felt more like Barry's big sister than his little one.

"I was having a hell of a time. I was angry at everybody. Almost lost my job, too. But I think I'm on a more even keel now."

Maddy watched her older brother eat for a few minutes, mixing her potato to mush before starting on it. He was a big guy, Viking material, with the blond, ruddy coloring to go with it. Both her brothers, Frank and Barry, had inherited the sky-blue eyes of their mother, while Maddy's were an indistinct blue-green-gray, reflecting whatever she was wearing.

Christmas had been a subdued affair for the entire family; she and her husband and children, and Frank and his new wife. They had all met at Maddy's house. After everyone had unwrapped their gifts, Barry's remained untouched under her tree, a silent reminder that he wasn't there.

It was better that he hadn't been there, Maddy knew. When Barry got depressed, he took it out on everyone around him. She hadn't made much of an effort to get him to come over Christmas Eve for the family dinner, knowing he would rejoin them when he was feeling more human. She knew he was spending nights at home, because his car would be there when she drove by to check.

Then, one bright Saturday in January, he appeared on her doorstep as if nothing had happened. She and Frank still didn't know who "Woody" was and how he had wronged their brother. Maybe they would never find out.

"I was having a personal problem." Barry looked up from his fries. "You know?"

"I can imagine," she said, although she couldn't. She knew that, even if she had identical relationship problems, as a heterosexual, it wasn't the same. Everything was harder for Barry. He had to face hostile attitudes and small persecutions, daily, on a scale she never would. The exclusions and slights she encountered as a member of the "weaker sex" paled in comparison to Barry's treatment.

His mood swings compounded everything, too. Maddy never knew which Barry she would encounter on any given day. She loved her brother and often wished life weren't so difficult for him. Would he have such violent ups and downs if he were straight?

"Things are great now, though," said Barry. "I'm back on my medicine and I've found the most wonderful person. We had a rough patch, but we're great now."

"Good for you, Barry." She was truly happy that he was doing so much better. "When do we get to meet him?"

"Not yet. He's not ready."

"Is your family so intimidating?" She smiled.

"No, no, it's not that. He's not 'out.'"

"Ah. Is he planning on coming out?"

"Oh sure, but he has to be ready. There are some complications. We'll work through it, though." He finished his burger and glanced at his watch. "Better get back to work. I'll call Frank tonight. See ya, sis."

Maddy smashed her fork into her potato again, then took a bite. It was cold. Maybe she'd find out who Woody was eventually, and maybe she wouldn't. Barry certainly wasn't going to tell her now. But he seemed so much happier and more stable.

She pecked Barry on the cheek when he leaned down as he left. Finally, things were getting back to normal. She would call Frank, just in case Barry didn't, happy to spread some good news after their dreary holidays.

Chapter 5

Hymn: A religious or sacred song.

The next board meeting felt better. Everyone greeted me, some remembered my name. I felt more relaxed because I wasn't thinking I had to make a good impression. The impression had already been made, good or bad. As the business of the group was discussed, though, I didn't know why I needed to be there. Maybe I would ask Roger if I had to attend every meeting. But later, not now when I was still so new.

I had spent the week going over and over the scores I would be conducting, and acquainting myself with the town. I'd also arranged and rearranged my few pieces of furniture a half dozen times. Soon, I hoped, Hopkins would feel like home. As we were leaving, Maddy stayed to chat. I learned that her two children were named Ethan and Emily. Ethan was in grade school and Emily in nursery school during this daytime board meeting. She didn't offer any explanation of the mysterious phone call during the last meeting, and I didn't ask. Didn't want to stick my nose in where it might not belong.

I was about to ask if she knew of any keyboard jobs when she asked me if I would like to sing at her Methodist church. "I know it's short notice," she said. "But tonight is choir rehearsal at my church. Would you like to join us?"

"Well, I sang in the church choir when I was in high school. I haven't since, for lack of time, but I love to sing."

"Come and try us out, if you want to." She gave me directions to the First United Methodist Church in Hopkins and said she would see me at seven.

I hadn't sung in a choir for so long I thought I'd better do some voice exercises as I pored over the musical scores. I warbled, "Wee-o wee-o wee-o wee-o wee, ya ya ya ya," and other nonsense syllables to stretch out my disused pipes.

Finally, in the late afternoon, I decided I'd better stop before I wore my voice out. I looked forward to meeting a new group of musicians and perhaps making some new friends. The only people I'd met besides Maddy were the other Chamber board members.

Wednesday evening I drove to the choir rehearsal through a sudden snowfall. In spite of Maddy's directions, I was confused. Two stone churches faced each other across the street. One proclaimed it was Presbyterian, so I turned into the one that said First United Methodist. Were there Second United Methodist churches?

Maddy had said to park near the rear door, since it was closer to the rehearsal room. Sure enough, a bunch of tire tracks led through the unshoveled parking lot to a small entry door. To get there, I had to drive past the outside of the large sanctuary, with impressive tall stained glass windows and a majestic steeple.

I pushed through the heavy back door and shook the snow off my boots. Maddy said the choir rehearsal room was at the near end of the main hall, with the sanctuary at the far end. The wetness from my boots puddled on the hallway floor, which was paved with tiny squares of gray mosaic tile.

Three rows of folding chairs were set up for rehearsal in the cramped room. A heavy-set man with wild carrot-colored hair and freckles stood before them, leafing through music at a conductor's stand.

Maddy spotted me and waved me over. "Sit by me," she said, patting the seat next to her.

"Is this the alto section?"

"Oh shoot, you sing alto?"

Maddy took me to the row behind hers and found me a seat there, with the other altos, and gave me some music and a folder.

"Hi," said the older woman next to me, sticking out her hand. She had beautiful dark eyes that slanted just slightly. They were dramatic in combination with her cropped, iron-gray hair. "My name's Olive Gaard. I'm the church secretary here. You must be the new chamber conductor Maddy told me about."

"Yes, I'm Cressa Carraway. I haven't sung in a choir for ages, so just poke me if I'm too loud, or way off."

The director banged his baton on his stand to get our attention.

"That's our Powell," Olive whispered.

"Okay," he said frowning. "Time to start. Sopranos warm up first."

Mr. Personality, I thought.

He gestured to the pianist at the spinet beside him, a thin nervous-looking man, who started noodling on the keys. The sopranos warbled with him, doing repeated series of notes progressively higher and higher until only a couple of voices were left. Then they were taken lower and lower. A tall redhead stood out, both in stature and voice. She gave Powell a smug look as she sang impossible-sounding high notes flawlessly, then winked at the pianist before the section sat down.

After the altos, tenors, and basses were taken through similar drills, we all stood up together and Powell took us through some arm and back stretches. Afterwards, we sat and started rehearsing the first song. We were doing a Natalie Sleeth piece and most of the people seemed to know their parts well. Olive whispered that they had been working on it for a few weeks and were singing it this coming Sunday.

It startled me when Powell—Mr. Personality—suddenly whanged his stick on the metal stand. We all stopped singing and most of us jumped. I gave a tiny yelp. The director was glaring at the accompanist sitting in front of the piano to his right.

"How can the altos sing the right note if you're playing the wrong one, Travis?"

"Sorry," he mumbled, ducking his head and looking daggers at Mr. P. We started the passage over, nervously.

The same sort of thing happened a couple more times, and once he berated a tenor for being a third off. His corrections were neither gentle nor kind, by any means. He was going for a no-hitter, determined that every pitch be perfect, every rhythm flawless. His corrections were needed, if the group was going to sing without mistakes, but his manner was extremely off-putting. Plus, a church choir doesn't achieve perfection every Sunday. Or any Sunday, usually. He reminded me of a conductor preparing for an important concert, one that would reflect on him and his career, rather than a church member trying to worship his god with the help of the singers.

I found myself thinking of my chamber group. I knew all of my musicians were volunteers, just like the church choir, and I sure wouldn't antagonize them. If they weren't enjoying what they were doing, they could go someplace else, and I'd be missing most of my musicians. I wondered how many singers the choir had lost because of their leader. That led me to wonder if I could get a conducting job here, as my second job. The thought only lasted a moment because I'd much rather conduct instruments. Vocal conducting is a whole 'nother ball game.

We went over some other anthems for future Sundays and then the director announced it was time for a break.

Olive stood up quickly and said she would like to introduce a new member first. "Powell, this is Cressa Carraway, who has just moved to Minneapolis. She's the new conductor of the Hopkins Chamber Ensemble. Cressa, our director, Powell Peckham."

So he *was* Mr. P.

Powell gave me a quick look and smile of interest, then stepped over to me and said he was happy to have me there.

He was a short, barrel-chested man with thin arms and legs. The way he used his hands in conducting was graceful, and he moved with a lightness that contradicted his bulk. His silky tenor voice had impressed me when he demonstrated some passages during the first half of rehearsal.

"Carraway," he repeated, giving me a curious glance. "I knew some Carraways once. I toured with them for a few months. Man and wife group."

I gulped, pained at their memory. They had died far too young. "Yes, they were probably my parents. Margit and Ryan?"

"That's them. Small world. I ran their sound. Good musicians. Did anyone ever learn more about the night they were killed?"

"What do you mean? It was an accident. Their car went off the road, on an icy patch somewhere in northern Minnesota. That's what I was told."

He was silent for a moment. "Nice to meet you," he mumbled and turned away.

Was he implying there was more to their deaths than an accident? Gram had hired a private investigator to delve further, and it was found to be just that, an accident. I'd even seen the final reports. She mentioned a letter from my parents had been missing, but Gram's note had made it quite clear that their deaths were accidental.

What did Powell mean about the night they died? He asked if I'd learned more. Did I learn more about what? I'd have to talk to him about that.

I followed Olive and the others into the hallway where one of the sopranos, who had ducked out a few minutes earlier, had set up a little metal cart with a coffee urn and Styrofoam cups for our break time. Maddy made her way over to where I stood by Olive. "How do you like it?" she asked me.

"I'll probably be croaking by the end of the night, I'm so out of practice, but it's fun to sing with a group again. Your choir sounds pretty good."

"I see you've met Olive," Maddy said to me, then turned to Olive.

"How's it going?" she asked.

"I'm enjoying sitting next to her," said Olive. "She reads so beautifully."

"Well, I am a professional musician," I said, trying for modesty. "I do read music well. My voice isn't the greatest, though. Not like my mother's was."

"I hope you're not too put off by Powell," said Maddy. "His bark is a lot worse than his bite."

"But it's not fun to be barked at either," retorted Olive. "My theory is, choir directors come and go, but the choir stays here. I'm waiting him out. We'll get a new conductor one of these days."

"And I was on the committee that hired him," said Maddy, making a sour face.

I wondered if Maddy liked being on committees.

"At least he hasn't started on Ingrid yet," Olive said.

"There's still time." Maddy screwed one corner of her mouth down and raised her eyebrows.

Powell appeared in the doorway and started herding us back into the rehearsal room.

The second half of rehearsal was even less pleasant than the first. Twice Powell stopped us and said that the sopranos were sharping—which they were, I could hear it. The second time, the tall, redheaded soprano huffed loudly and glared at Powell with an angry expression.

"Uh-oh," whispered Olive. "Here we go again."

The third time we stopped, Powell said, "Ingrid, please! Try to stay on pitch!"

"I'm not the one off pitch," the tall redhead shot back.

"I can prove you are," he spat. "Drop out for five minutes and your section will sound just fine."

"I can drop out for the rest of the night!" she shouted and flounced out the door, bumping against the chair of a bass singer on her way.

"Smells like she's drunk," the bass puffed, under his breath. "A choir of drunks and fags." He gave a disgusted sniff. I don't think too many people in the choir could hear him. I hoped not.

Travis jumped up from the piano bench and followed Ingrid.

"Travis is Ingrid's husband," Olive whispered to me. "And Powell always yells at her, but this is the first time she's left rehearsal."

Travis returned a minute later and resumed his seat, glaring at Powell, his thin lips tight.

Powell blew out his breath, then said, "Let's do Sunday's anthem one more time."

We did it, not very joyously, then rehearsal was over. The mood in the room was so foul I put off talking to Powell about my parents and left the room as soon as I could. At least I had met a new friend, so I now had two friends in Minnesota, Maddy and Olive.

Chapter 6

Comodetto: Rather easily or leisurely (Ital.)

Thursday was a brilliant sunny day. The light snowfall from the day before ran in sparkling streams beside the roads. The street in front of my building had a bicycle path beside it, as did most of the streets in the area. It was the first day without snow or a threat of snow, so I got on my bike. I found a meat market just down the street and around the corner, where they made their own bratwurst. The plump sausages made my mouth water, anticipating the spicy, salty taste, so I bought a couple and headed for the door, watching out for wet spots on the slick tile floor.

"Oops, sorry." I looked up at the woman I bumped into with my head down. It was Ingrid, the six-foot redhead from choir. She was entering the shop, heading toward the counter. She wasn't happy.

She continued walking forward for a minute, deep into conversation on the cell phone at her ear. "You're no help, you know, sis? All you can think about is your wedding. Wedding, huh." She sniffed. "I wish I'd never gotten married. At least not to Travis."

Then she turned with belated recognition. "Oh. Hi. Cressa, isn't it?" she gulped. "Hang on a sec," she said to the cell phone. "I'll call you back."

Tears trickling from her deep blue eyes dripped onto her coat collar.

"Are you okay?" was my rather stupid question. Of course she wasn't okay—she was crying.

Ingrid sniffed. "I don't know what to do."

"Are you and Travis having problems?"

"Are we ever! I'm sorry, I don't want to bother you. And I'd rather not talk about it."

That seemed to be the end of that subject.

"Sure, no problem. I hope something works out." Boy, I sounded lame.

I left her to her meat purchase and pedaled back to my apartment, splashing through the tiny spontaneous rivers of snow melt that gurgled alongside the curbs. I started humming a little bit of Schubert's "Trout Quintet," probably because of its watery theme.

I stopped to look at the little pond at my complex, but didn't stay long because the benches were wet with melting snow and there was no place to sit. The pond was mostly frozen over, but a patch near the shore was ice-free. Several mallards paddled around and around in the icy cold water and I wondered if their efforts were what was keeping the ice from forming, or if there was maybe a little warm spring at the bottom of the pond.

Back at the apartment, I found I could put off the rest of my unpacking just a little longer. I called Daryl, but in the middle of the day, he was teaching. I left a message saying all was fine and I was missing him. We'd only talked twice since I'd arrived in Minnesota. The rest of the week we'd missed each other's calls.

Our conversations were strained and, on his end, hurried. I tried to tell him how much I was looking forward to being a real conductor instead of a school one, but he didn't want to hear me. He was usually full of news about the projects he was working on, but I couldn't get him to tell me anything about them.

Roger had given me a key to the high school where our rehearsals would be, and I could tell, by the school buses putt-putting by, that school had let out. Here was another way to put my unpacking off.

I got into my car and drove over to the high school to scout out the chamber orchestra rehearsal space. My little blue Chevy Cruze felt so much more comfortable than the Toyota I'd been renting. When I knew I had this job, I had bought it used and retired my even older jalopy.

I climbed onto the podium, but found I was too afraid of looking silly to actually wave my arms around conducting. What if someone saw me?

The room we would be using was designed solely for orchestra rehearsal, not a band hall that served double duty as is the case in many high schools. This meant that there were no built-in risers. Since we would be performing on the flat, it was better to rehearse on the flat. Our group wasn't big enough to need risers for the players in the rear to be able to see me. I wished our first rehearsal—next Monday—weren't so far off.

When I returned to the apartment this time, there were two messages on the land line phone that came with the apartment. One was from Maddy Streete, inviting me to lunch on Saturday. The other was from Roger Hirt, the handsome conductor from the Chamber Board, inviting me to dinner on Friday.

There were no messages from Darryl.

"Guess I'd better cook my sausages tonight," I said to the machine as I picked up the receiver to accept both of my invitations. I was getting more than a little irritated with Daryl. The hell with him. I lived here now and he lived there.

Joshua vowed for the, like, maybe twentieth time to clean up. He was so damn tired of living like this. He made the cold trek to the shelter where they told him the chaplain would be in shortly.

The chairs in the hallway were hard and wooden, but it was warm at least. When the chaplain talked to him, he would tell him about his plans to clean up. Sober up. Quit stealing and get a job. True, he wasn't quite sober at the moment, but he intended to be soon.

What did they expect? No one paid any attention to him. He hadn't seen his father for three years, not that he wanted to. Stupid fag. The memory of "that day" started playing in his head again. The memory was one of the reasons he did smack. Sometimes the drugs stopped the endless loop of That Day. Sometimes they didn't.

That Day.

Ma had just gotten home from work and Josh was watching music videos on YouTube. "Turn those off, Josh," she called from the kitchen, "and come help me with this."

Okay, okay. He muted the video and shambled into the kitchen.

"Listen, hon, while I get changed you put the salad together. It's a special night, our anniversary, and I want to have a nice dinner for your dad. We'll probably go out this weekend, but this is the actual day."

She pecked him on his shaggy head and disappeared into the master bedroom. She was happier than she'd been these last few months and it lightened his heart.

Josh was able to shred the lettuce at the end of the counter and still see into the den where the computer silently wound through the next video. He just finished the greens and was slicing some radishes when Dad came through the back door into the kitchen.

"Hi, Sport," he said.

Josh grunted.

"Hey, I said 'hi'," Dad protested.

"Hi." Josh grinned and looked up at him.

"Whacha doin'?"

"Duh, I'm making the salad. Ma said it's a special night."

Dad took a deep breath. "Well, I guess it is," he said almost to himself. He straightened his shoulders and headed to the bedroom. He didn't look like he was looking forward to celebrating, Josh thought.

It wasn't very long—Josh was slicing mushrooms—before he heard raised angry voices. He stopped working. Frowning, he listened, coldness stealing into his heart.

"How could you?" screamed his mother, over and over, louder and louder. "How could you, how could you!"

"Laura, please."

"No, just get out." She sounded hysterical.

This went on for several minutes, Dad pleading and Ma shrill, while Joshua held his breath and stood motionless, not seeing the videos any more. The chill in his heart turned to a lump of ice in his stomach. Then their voices stopped and, after a few minutes of silence, Dad trudged out of the bedroom, through the kitchen, and out the back door.

He heard his mother weeping. He plunked down and sat at the kitchen table, not knowing what to do. Finally, after about a half an hour—maybe more, it was hard to tell—she came into the kitchen.

"Josh, baby." She looked terrible. Her eyes were red and her face was all saggy. "Josh, how can I tell you?"

"What, what?"

She sat beside him and patted his arm awkwardly. Since he had become a teenager there hadn't been a lot of touching. Not like when he was a little kid and used to sit in her lap every night.

"Where did Dad go?"

Her face turned hard and her voice had an edge. "Don't ever talk about him again, you hear?"

What? Not talk about Dad? He knew they fought sometimes. Lately, they mostly ignored each other, just kind of lived in the same house. But still. She was Ma and he was Dad.

"He's not your father anymore."

Josh's eyes grew big. "Huh?" His mind reeled.

"This is really hard to say. You know we haven't been getting along. Right?"

Josh nodded.

"I thought maybe he was seeing another woman. I've asked him and asked him about it. So today he finally told me." She looked down at the table, and her eyes held such profound sadness it scared Josh. "He *has* been seeing someone else." Her voice came out in a whisper. "It's a man. He's seeing a man."

The world wheeled. The room spun. It even seemed like the lights dimmed.

They sat there at the kitchen table for hours, the forlorn salad wilting, and cried until their eyes were dry, out of tears. Then Joshua went to bed, his world forever changed.

Chapter 7

Overro: Or; or else (Ital.)

The Saturday luncheon took place at a little coffee shop on Ridgedale Drive, not far from my apartment. Maddy picked me up. I was waiting outside so she wouldn't have to see the state of my apartment. I had been unpacking for days, but when I looked around dispassionately there were lots of boxes left.

I was still avoiding unpacking. Instead, I had spent a lot of time poring over the ever-present scores the day before, then had spent hours getting ready for my dinner with Roger. The board, or maybe Roger, had picked the music for the first concert so I didn't have to (or didn't get to) pick the program.

The coffee shop Maddy took me to had excellent sandwiches that came in a reasonable size. We munched and chatted for a few minutes about the improving weather and the slushy road conditions—I learned that seeing the sun for two days in a row in January is quite remarkable for Minnesota—then Maddy leaned forward slightly. "I want to explain about Powell," she said. "I feel kind of bad about the whole situation."

"What do you mean?" I asked, thinking of the embarrassing bickering I had witnessed.

"Well, the choir's kind of a mess right now. Maybe I shouldn't have dragged you into it. Most of the members want to get rid of Powell. And I feel responsible because I was on the SPR when he was hired."

"SP...what's that?"

"SPR. It stands for Staff Parish Relations, sort of like Human Resources. We're the people in the church who decide who gets raises, hire and fire people. We're accountable to the whole church, of course, and it *is* a committee, so we usually make fairly reasonable decisions. Although we did hire a youth director a few years ago—thank God I wasn't on the committee then—who had problems with inappropriate behavior, but he was out fast." She slurped her empty iced tea glass.

"Hey, you're on the committee that hired me, too."

She smiled. "Different committee. We have tons of committees in the church, only one for the chamber group. And I know you'll work out better than Powell. Want a refill?" She jumped up and got our free refills from the tea urns at the back of the room.

"Really, don't apologize," I said when she returned. "I'm enjoying the singing. And Powell *is* a good musician."

"Yes, he is. Everybody loved him when he first started. The choir director before him never did anything new—we always sang boring anthems we could sing in our sleep." She traced circles in the sweat on her glass. "But Powell wanted us to be as good as we could possibly be. At least, that's the way it started. Now I think he wants us to be better than we can possibly be."

"Sounds like a problem." I sipped the yummy peach-flavored iced tea.

"Oh, there's more, believe me," she said. "Travis, the organist, is on the verge of quitting—he talked to the committee recently. I'll be surprised if Ingrid comes back. This week's rehearsal might have been the last straw for both of them. And three other sopranos and two altos have already dropped out because of him."

"Ouch. That's not good." That answered my question about whether or not they were losing members.

"No, it isn't. But you know how people in a church feel about a choir director they don't like, don't you?"

I shook my head.

"The usual view," she said, "is that the choir will always be there, but directors come and go. Some people, the ones that have dropped out, will be back when Powell is gone. Directors are usually temporary."

I had heard Olive say the same thing. "That's the same way people feel about community bands and orchestras. The pit orchestra I played with in high school had a second violin player who was famous for playing with every other conductor."

Maddy nodded. "I kept hoping Powell would settle in a little better, get to know people and be able to work with them. The whole committee hoped that. But he just wants to bully us. And the worst of it is, I think his main goal is to make himself look good."

"I haven't seen much of him, of course, but I'll have to agree with you on that last one. Seems to me he's treating the group like they were paid professionals instead of volunteers. It's like his goal is a perfect performance. That's fine if lots of people are paying money to hear you sing, but in a church, everyone's in it together. No one minds a few bobbles in the choir."

Maddy nodded, "The main thing is to help the congregation praise God. That's what a church choir is really for. The spirit should be cooperation." She sighed and picked up her iced tea glass. "What a mess!"

"And what about that bass? He was making rude comments when Ingrid left. Something about fags and drunks."

Maddy took a deep breath, and just then the waitress stopped by to take our credit cards. After she left, Maddy pursed her lips and shook her head. "Good old Arthur Alexander. Alexander the Great, we call him. He's ex-military—a sergeant or something—thinks it gives him authority over everybody. More than once he's voiced the opinion that Powell is, as he puts it, a fag. I think he's one of those macho guys that are scared to death of gay people. And, actually, I do think Ingrid was a little tipsy Wednesday night. I was sitting two seats away. I got some fumes when she faced my way."

Maddy's cell phone regaled us with *Für Elise* and she dove into her purse to retrieve it just as I was going to mention bumping into Ingrid at the meat market. She hadn't seemed tipsy that day. Just teary.

"'Scuse me a minute. I'm expecting this one."

She said hello and listened for a while, then sighed deeply. "Okay, just let me know. Promise? I love you." She ended the call and let her breath out. "That was my brother, Barry. He just canceled a date for dinner at our house for tonight. He was supposed to bring someone over for my family to meet, but, apparently, they're on the outs again."

I gave a noncommittal *Hmm*.

"He'll be the death of me," she said. "He's always either up or down, never in the middle. One of those extreme people. Kind of hard to live with. Like Powell."

"Problems, problems," I said, trying to sound sympathetic. "Well, be sure to let me know if the organist gives notice."

"Why? Do you want Travis's job?"

Did I? I sure wouldn't want to work with Perfect Powell, so probably no. "I'm going to have to find something to supplement my income. I've been thinking about applying around to see if any local churches need a pianist or an organist. I could do either or both. My undergraduate major was keyboard performance."

"Sure," she said. "I'll be happy to at least let you apply for the job. But I don't think you'd want to work with Powell, right?"

"Probably not." I gave a sigh. "Want to talk about something completely different? Well, it does involve a conductor."

"What?" She looked at me with a puzzled smile.

"I went to dinner with Roger Hirt last night."

"I knew it!" She laughed.

"What do you mean?"

"I don't know. It just seemed like he was more interested in you than, um, just pretty interested. What did you think of him?"

"He's friendly, down to earth. Doesn't seem to have the Hitler/Napoleon mentality that some conductors have, like Powell, for instance. He's good looking, that's for sure."

Maddy nodded. "And?"

"Tell me one thing. Why isn't he attached? At his age?"

She paused and looked at me directly. "He just got divorced a few months ago. His wife was a flute player in the Minnesota Orchestra—you know he's a trombonist with them? In addition to being the Minnetonka Symphony conductor?"

"Yeah, he told me all that. What about the ex-wife?" At least I wouldn't be getting involved with a married man. I'd done that once before and it was a fiasco.

"She got a job in New York and took off. The rumor is that there was a percussionist involved."

"You gotta watch those drummers," I said, laughing, remembering that the drummers were always the bad boys in high school band.

"Any kids?" I asked.

"Nope."

"Good." I smiled, feeling smug, then chagrined. "What am I saying? I have a boyfriend back in Chicago."

"What's his name?"

"Daryl Johannson. I must say he's not burning up the phone lines since I moved. But neither am I."

I didn't know what was happening between Daryl and me since I moved. When I left for this job, I made it clear that I wasn't leaving him... didn't I? He didn't make it clear that *he* wasn't leaving me, though.

If I dated someone else, would that straighten my thinking out, show me whether I wanted to stay with Daryl or not?

Lots of questions...

After we finished signing our checks, I said, "So, back to Powell. Are you really going to have to fire him?"

"Probably. Our committee doesn't meet for a couple of weeks, so nothing will happen right away. Church committees usually move like glaciers. And we have all the rules of a human resources department. Powell has been given his three warnings. We've tried to sit down with him and talk, but he's not very receptive to comments, let alone criticism."

Maddy made a what-can-you-do face. "If we do decide to let him go, we'll have to find a new director. That's a brand new headache. Oh well, this is my last year on SPR. I don't think I'll ever volunteer for that committee again!"

After she dropped me off, I decided I would have to buckle down and practice conducting the scores for my first rehearsal, which would be on Monday night. Two days away. *Yikes!*

What on earth was I thinking, talking to her about Roger that way? I had a perfectly good boyfriend back in Chicago. Daryl and I had gone through a lot, and there was nothing wrong with Daryl—except that he wasn't here.

Or at least, that's what I told myself.

The phone rang. It was Neek, breathless on the other end. "Cressa. This is a good one, but I don't understand it at all."

"Okay, I'll bite. What did you find now?"

"It's quartz! I think it means you're going to find a new love."

I gulped. "A new love? Here, I guess?" *Roger?* He was kind to me and good-looking, but I didn't know much about him. I didn't even know if he had any feelings for me.

"But what about Daryl? Aren't you still with Daryl?"

"Well, yeah. I mean, we're not living very close, but…"

"See, that's what I don't get. Do you think he's going to dump you? Or—Omigosh! Are *you* dumping him?"

"To tell you the truth, Neek, I'm not sure what's going on right now. We're not communicating very well. I don't think he hears me when I tell him how much this new position means to me. He seems to think I should play at it awhile, then come back to teaching."

"I didn't think you liked teaching."

"See? That's what I mean. You know that, and I know that, but Daryl doesn't get it. You're right, I hate teaching. I won't do it again unless I absolutely have to."

"Well, I *did* find a piece of quartz today. And it was right where you always used to park your car."

"Maybe it pertains to the person who parks there now?"
"No! I have a *feeling,* Cressa."

After we hung up, I stood with my hand on the phone for several minutes. What, exactly, was going on with me and Daryl? I had no business going out with Roger when we hadn't broken up. I wasn't, I told myself, that kind of girl. I would either have to make Daryl understand I was here and not moving back to Chicago for the time being, or we would have to take a breather. But just up and seeing another guy was not fair. Furious with myself and my obvious tendency for duplicity, I plunked myself down and got out the score I had been slaving over. Music, my familiar refuge.

I practiced cueing the lower strings in the Sarabande, trying to hear all the complicated threads of the piece in my head, wondering why Bach bothered to include the flute in this movement, since it was exactly the same as the first violin. But I was glad he did write it that way, otherwise there would be even more threads to keep straight.

I also needed to study the rest of the program, although the other pieces weren't nearly so demanding. We were playing a version of the Prayer from Humperdinck's *Hansel and Gretel,* plus two Pleyel suites. I wouldn't have programmed the concert with these. The group had a talented flautist, needed for the Bach, but the Humperdinck and the Pleyel didn't use the flute at all. Since she was needed for the Bach, I would have picked other pieces that also used flute. Besides, as I remembered from my audition, she was a damn good flute player.

According to Maddy, someone in the community had recently donated the Bach music to the chamber group, so it was imperative that we play it. That was no problem, since I loved the B Minor Suite. The last movement is a joyous outburst of typical Bach energy, and is often heard in many forms, played by lots of different instruments, including cell phones. What's amazing to me is that all this buoyant energy is in a minor key! Minor keys are supposed to sound sad, as opposed to major-happy keys. Usually minors are used for doleful, mournful, or at least sweet, longing pieces. But Bach can burst forth in any key.

I was conscious that I needed to be picking pieces for the rest of the season, though. The programming for the first concert was decided before I was hired, but it was up to me to fill the rest of the bills. I wondered vaguely if we should have an all-Bach program later. I didn't get anywhere in my decision making, so I returned to the B Minor Suite.

After I had reviewed the Sarabande movement several times, I was still not getting myself coordinated in the conducting. I threw down my new baton, but not too hard—didn't want to break it—and picked up the phone. Then something strange happened.

I meant to call Roger. I wanted to confer with him on programming in general, since I couldn't make myself decide anything, but my fingers dialed Daryl's number. Not surprising, since I didn't have Roger's memorized. But when Daryl answered, it startled me.

"Daryl?" I said, stupidly.

"Cressa? Yeah, it's me. Haven't heard from you for a while, but I've been gone a lot. My new showing opens next weekend, and I'm still finishing one more piece that I want to include. Crazy, huh?"

"Hi. Yeah, I've been busy, too."

"I tried to call last night."

Silence. I couldn't think of what to say. I couldn't tell him I'd been out to dinner with a good-looking single man. Or that his number wasn't in my caller ID.

"Glad your show's going well," I said.

"Going well? It's not opening until Saturday. I just told you, I'm still trying to finish one more piece for it."

"Oh, yeah. You did say that."

"Are you okay?"

"I'm just fine. I'm a little tired." Not true at all.

"Well, glad you called. I'm doing fine. When's your first rehearsal?"

"Monday. I'm really nervous about it. Nervous, but excited. And I've met a lot of great people. I even went to sing in a church choir last week." I fingered the locket on the chain around my neck, my prized possession. When I touched the smooth metal, my tension lowered. I could even feel my shoulders relax. The locket was from my dear Gram who passed away a little over a year ago, and the chain was from Daryl.

"Oops, there's the timer for the stove. Look, I'll call you later."

"Okay," I said, but he had already hung up. I tried to remember whether or not his stove had a timer.

Chapter 8

Voci: Plural of Voce: Voice; part (Ital.)

Melvin Tucker, senior pastor of the First United Methodist church, gathered the skirts of his black robe as he ascended into his pulpit on Sunday morning. This was his element: when he was here, looking down on the congregation, he felt he was where he belonged. Maybe it was a bit arrogant, a bit prideful. But he loved the feeling that he was the leader, the shepherd. The symbolism of standing above the rest of the congregants was, he told himself, secondary to the practicality of being where he could be seen and heard as he preached God's word.

He much preferred preaching over all the other aspects of ministering. Counseling had to be his least favorite task. He was sometimes at a loss for words before the profound sadness and inhumanity that was related to him in the small confines of his office. Sometimes he felt that there wasn't enough air in the room when heartbreak rolled off the lips of his flock members.

But now he was in his pulpit. Today the sermon was on the first miracle of Jesus, turning the water to wine at the wedding in Cana. It was one of his favorite texts because so much human detail was provided in the gospel of John about this event.

John 2:1-11 was one of the lectionary texts for this Sunday, the second Sunday after Epiphany. Since Melvin had been preaching for so many years, he turned to the lectionary for his subjects less and less. He often used the ones for January, however, because they contained some of his favorite Bible passages. This one gave him a lot to work with.

It was easy to vividly reconstruct the scene. Among other points, he built on Jesus's resistance to his mother's lament about being out of wine, and her implication that he should do something about it. Then his mother, in typical mom-fashion, ignores his misgivings and proceeds as if he is going to follow her instructions. Which, of course, he does. Then the best part—the guests remarking about how much better this wine is than the stuff they were drinking before. He drew the word pictures elegantly, waving his robed arms toward the gathering as he helped the congregation to envision the details of the scene, the jars of wine, the buffet table, and the guests.

His gaze swept the sanctuary as he spoke. There was Carmella, his wife, in the third row, as always. She had perfected the look of rapt attention. Melvin never knew whether it was real or affected, but liked to assume the former.

Ginny Dahlberg sat on the left-most aisle, halfway back, a slight frown creasing her pretty forehead. He knew that as director of the nursery school she dealt with a thousand little problems weekly. Usually, she handled each crisis with aplomb, but the Barry issue was getting to her.

Barry Slade, the one who wanted the nursery school out of the church for some reason, sat on the far right. His attention was not riveted on the sermon. Rather, he alternated between gazing at the chandeliers hanging from the beams overhead and bending down to inspect the terrazzo floor. When Barry had requested a private counselling session, Melvin had met with Barry several times in private, not feeling that he could offer him much help. But just listening seemed to do Barry a lot of good. He hadn't made up his mind yet whether giving Barry the trustee job had been a good idea or not. It was probably good for Barry—he hoped it would be—but was it good for the church? At any rate, Barry needed another session soon.

There were a few people Melvin used as Interest Gauges, but Barry wasn't one of them since his moods were unpredictable. Arthur Alexander in the choir was nodding off and softly snoring, as usual, so he couldn't be used, either. The most reliable barometer was Paula, who sat in the third row, usually near his wife. If Paula looked interested, he knew his message was getting out. On the other hand, if she started fidgeting and leafing through the hymnal, he knew he had to step up the volume and the hand gestures just a mite. Sometimes, he even deviated from his text and threw in a joke from the list he kept with his sermon notes. They were holy, or holy-ish jokes. He preferred not to have to resort to them.

Today, Paula cocked her head and paid attention. Good. This one was going over.

Melvin drew two lessons from the miracle story. First, the flock should always be prepared to follow the shepherd. Second, sometimes the best is saved for last. He liked simple, easy-to-understand messages. They were received better than convoluted, intellectual interpretations of things he dimly understood and would be lost on everyone else in the congregation.

Satisfied with his homily, he took his place on the minister's bench behind the pulpit and nodded to Powell Peckham: the choir should begin the anthem.

The rolling three-four rhythm of Sleeth's "Hymn of Promise" soothed and pleased Melvin. A smile stole over his face as he shut his eyes and felt the rocking of his sailboat in his mind. The song was about seasons, and summer was Melvin's favorite. In Minnesota it can be a short season, but the lakes teem with sailors, fishers, swimmers, and water-skiers.

He pictured his new Catalina. Well, new to him. He had purchased it used at the end of last summer and only taken it out once. It would be nice to sail it with Willard, his colleague and the pastor at the Presbyterian church across the street. Willard used to be a good sailor and Olive, Melvin's secretary, kept telling him that Willard needed some attention.

Guilt washed over him for not calling Willard lately. But then, Willard hadn't called him, either. He knew Willard was still experiencing a lot of pain over his wife's death. In fact, last summer, on that one outing with Melvin's new boat, Willard had been so distracted he could hardly handle the sails. Maybe he should find a new sailing partner. No, that was not the charitable thing to do. Willard was in pain and needed friends. Another wave of guilt poured over Melvin, and he vowed to call Willard that very afternoon.

Powell was looking at him. Ah, the choir was done singing. The Reverend Melvin Tucker got slowly to his feet to lead the congregation in reciting the Apostles' Creed.

Chapter 9

Forzando: With force, energy (Ital.)

The choir rehearsal room was a noisy place after the service, even without Powell Peckham's brief tirade. Everyone hushed after he left. I hung back and let the others hang up their robes, then put mine on its assigned, numbered hanger on the long clothes pole at the side of the room. I made my way to the back where wooden shelves lined the wall. As I stuck my choir folder into my cubby hole, Olive tapped me on the shoulder.

"Meet me in my office," she whispered. Puzzled, I waited to let some other choir members pass in front of me, and made my way up the stairs. The church office was straight ahead as you entered the building and mounted the stone steps from the front door. A landing from that door led down to the basement. The sanctuary was to the right at the top of the stairs.

She motioned me in and shut the door.

Seeing my quizzical look, she explained. "This is the only private place to talk on a Sunday morning, and I wanted your opinion. How do you think it went?"

"I think it was fine." I assumed she meant the singing of the anthem by the choir. "Even though Ingrid did sharp on the loud part, Powell's tirade in the choir room afterward was way overboard. I'm sure ninety-nine percent of the congregation thought it was lovely. 'Hymn of Promise' is so beautiful, it's hard to ruin it."

"That's for sure."

"And what's with that guy you call Alexander the Great? The bass with the chip on his shoulder? He was in rare form."

Olive shrugged, raising her eyebrows with her shoulders. "I know. He sleeps through the sermon, then he misses his entrance because he sings with his face buried in his music."

I chuckled. "I hadn't noticed all that. But I did witness his little snit in the choir room. Swatting at Powell and telling him not to touch him."

"Well, Powell ought to know better than to put an arm around that one." Olive sighed.

"But that's not why I called you in here." Her beautiful oval eyes lit up. "I was talking on Friday to Trudy, the secretary at Hopkins Heights Presbyterian church. You know, the one right across the street?"

I nodded. I'd noticed it. It was a handsome brick building with a tall, slim bell tower. This street was a Church Row, with two more churches across from each other a block away.

"She said," Olive continued, "that Sharon, their organist, is pregnant with twins. They had a substitute lined up for her when she takes maternity leave, but she'll have to quit sooner than anyone thought. Maddy told me—"

We heard raised voices in the hallway outside the office door. A man's harsh, angry voice shouted, "Just a minute. Don't walk away when I'm trying to talk to you."

A woman's voice answered him, trembling and high-pitched. "If you don't leave me alone, I'll—"

"What? Hold on a minute. Look, just hold still. I have to tell you this."

A thirty-something attractive blond woman burst through the door, followed by a large red-faced man who was shaking his fist at her.

The poor woman looked half-way between angry and scared, and walked with her head down. When she raised her face, she spied us and stopped. We must have encouraged her because she turned to face him.

I tried to look small, not wanting to share the brunt of the man's anger. There was a counter that ran halfway across the room between us.

"If this was the first time it ever happened, it'd be different," the man went on, oblivious to his audience. "The second grade Sunday School teacher complains to me every week."

"And how many other teachers complain?" Her voice was steadier now than it had been in the hallway. She drew herself up taller.

He stopped and considered, lowering his tone a little. "I guess she's the only one."

"Well, then, I don't think it's a huge problem, do you?" Her reasonable, restrained manner made it seem she was talking to a child. "I will be sure and tell Deborah that there is one particular Sunday School teacher who, though she is so picky we couldn't possibly please her, insists that the nursery school leave the room immaculate every single week. What did you say was the problem? Crayon marks on the table?"

"Crayon markings, sticky tables, your painting equipment stored on the wrong shelf. The Sunday School gets the top two shelves, you only get the bottom one." The man flung one arm out, then the other, indicating shelves, I guessed.

"Listen, Barry," she said, evenly, stepping back out of range of his flying hands, "Second graders need a lot of equipment. We can't possibly fit everything on one shelf. And your Sunday School people don't use half of the top shelf."

The man glared at her, spun around, and stalked out.

"Are you okay, Ginny?" asked Olive, approaching her.

Ginny's confidence crumpled and she turned to Olive, shaking with silent sobs. "Why can't he just leave me alone?"

Olive guided her around the counter to her own office chair and got her seated. "That was totally uncalled for," agreed Olive, patting her shoulder. "I'll speak to Pastor Melvin about it and see if he can talk some sense into Barry. Everyone knows what Vanessa is like. She's an impossible neatnik.

"I remember her at church suppers when she was little, crying because the edges of her food were touching. Her mother had to use a plate with little ridges to separate her food at home, and she even brought her special plate to church dinners. I think Vanessa outgrew that, but she didn't outgrow being an annoying brat."

I cringed, hearing a church secretary gossip like that, but it seemed to cheer Ginny up.

"Oh, Cressa," said Olive, turning to me. "Meet Ginny Dahlberg, the director of the nursery school that meets here during the week. As you may have gathered, they share classrooms with the Sunday School. How many years have you been here, Ginny?"

"Twelve, going on thirteen." She looked proud of those years.

"And there's never been any conflict about the space before these last few weeks. Don't worry, Ginny. We can work this out. I promise I'll talk to Melvin first thing Tuesday. Monday is his day off."

Ginny sniffled. "Oh, Olive. It's only going to get worse. The teachers, and the parents, too, have been after me to expand the program to five days a week instead of three. Barry will fight us every inch of the way."

"You have a lot of backers in the church, Ginny. Almost everyone else will stand behind you."

"But," Ginny stopped and let out a long breath, then continued. "I don't know if I can fight him right now."

"Why?" said Olive. "What's the problem?" Olive perched on the edge of her desk. The top was empty of papers except for a stack of a few sheets in the middle. If that were my desk I knew I wouldn't be able to find a place to perch. I leaned against the counter, feeling that I maybe shouldn't be there.

"I'm going to announce it at the board meeting this Thursday, but I'll tell you now. Don't tell a soul, though. I don't want it being put into the rumor mill any sooner than it has to be."

I hunched my head down a bit, really, really not wanting to be here.

Olive gave me a quick glance, but Ginny continued as though I weren't there. "I have breast cancer."

We both gasped and my head came up.

"I'm having surgery two weeks from Monday. After that, I don't know how long I'll be laid up."

"Ginny," whispered Olive, grabbing her hand.

"I know," Ginny went on, "that Nicole will be able to handle everything until I'm back. And I'll be available for her, of course. But this thing with Barry."

Olive's pretty, tilted eyes grew steely. "I want you to go home and just worry about your health. I promise that, between Melvin and me, we'll handle Barry. Whatever's gotten into him is going to have to get out."

Olive handed her a tissue from the box on the counter and Ginny dried her eyes and left, thanking Olive tearfully for her help.

My shoulders sagged, so did Olive's, and we both gave totally inappropriate nervous little giggles.

"Hard to believe Barry is Maddy's brother," she muttered. "Looks like he's gone off the deep end again. I'll phone to Melvin tonight. He'll know what to do. Okay. Now why did we come in here?"

She ran a hand through her short, metal-colored hair.

"You were telling me about the organist across the street."

"Oh yes. Maddy told me you were looking for an organist job and, with theirs taking maternity leave, there's an opening there at Hopkins Heights."

"That's great! I haven't really started looking, just been thinking about it. But, really? That guy is Maddy's brother?"

She nodded. "He's the new head of the Trustees."

"Trusties?" I asked. "Like in prison?"

"No, no," she smiled. "Like in the committee that takes care of the building and grounds. I've always liked Barry, but he's been acting *so* weird lately. I have no idea what's wrong with him, but something—I don't know, something is."

I hesitated, then asked her, "Do churches always have this much conflict going on? I mean, the tension in the choir is so tight you can almost strum it, and then these two."

"Wherever you have people, you have conflict," she answered. "Just because it's a church doesn't mean it's all sweetness and light. A church is made up of people. Most folks here get along, most of the time. I admit we're having a string of problems right now. They come in waves, I guess." She straightened the papers on her desk, which were already perfectly straight.

"But you're interested in the organist job? That's good. If you're half as good an organist as you are a singer—"

"Better, I hope. After all, I've actually studied organ. Do you think it's a good place to work?"

"Better than this one right now, I would guess. You can talk to Travis about them. He's subbed there several times, especially in the last few months when Sharon wasn't up to it. He's marvelous on the organ, can step right up on a moment's notice. He studied in France when he was younger."

Lucky Travis. My training was All-American, but I'd put it up against his on the organ. Maybe the piano, too. "What does First do for an organist when Travis plays there?"

"We have the bell choir perform, or the choir can sing *a capella* when he's gone. Plus we have several piano players in the congregation that can play the hymns. It's nice to give others a chance when he's gone."

Olive copied down the phone number of Trudy, the secretary at the neighboring Presbyterian church, and sent me on my way.

A wrinkled hand touched my arm as I reached for my car door.

"Sorry, didn't mean to scare you." It was the irascible bass, Arthur Alexander, the one who didn't care for "fags and drunks."

"I heard Powell talking to you Wednesday," he said. His voice was low. Not rumbly, but raspy, like he was or had been a smoker. He spoke loudly enough for the whole parking lot to hear, if anyone else had been there.

"Yes?" I lowered my arm and his hand dropped off.

"About your parents."

I waited for him to continue.

"I didn't want to have to say this, but…"

Again, he stopped. Would he ever get to the point? Maybe I could help him. "He said he worked with them as a sound technician. A few months, he said."

"What do you know about the night they died?" he asked.

Now he had my full attention. "I know they died in a car wreck on an icy road after a New Year's Eve gig. Why, what do *you* know?"

"The road was icy, all right. But that ice was put there. They didn't tell you that, did they?"

He stalked off.

"Wait!" I shouted after him, but he slipped into his car and drove off, ignoring me as if we had never spoken.

Driving home, I pondered his words and decided not to put too much credence in what he implied, which was that the death of my parents was not completely an accident. Whether it was or not, they'd been dead for many years.

An old wound opened just a tad, though. The guilt I had felt when they died. I hadn't been sad, hadn't grieved. In the years before they died, I hadn't seen them often. I lived with my grandparents and they were more like my parents. I felt guilty for not missing the mother and father I had barely known.

Smoothly, almost unconsciously—I had done it so many times—I buried those thoughts and sealed that wound back up. I turned my thoughts to the present and the scene I had just witnessed.

I tried to picture Maddy, whom I liked very much, beside Barry, whom I had instantly disliked. Remembering, though, that my Gram always used to say that you can't pick your relatives, I decided not to hold the behavior of her brother against Maddy.

My very first rehearsal of my very first orchestra was happening tomorrow night and, even though I had studied and studied and *studied* the Bach score, I still didn't feel completely prepared. Maybe I never would.

Chapter 10

Stentando: Dragging (Ital.)

I was in my apartment about fifteen minutes before the land-line phone rang, long enough to kick off my shoes and pour a glass of wine. I was surprised to hear Roger's voice when I picked up.

"How'd the first rehearsal go?" he said. He sounded genuinely interested, and his voice resonated over the telephone.

"I'm just glad it's over." I sighed and took a sip of my wine. "I enjoyed it after I got going, but I was so nervous the first half hour. It's kind of like giving a speech—and way, way worse than playing a solo. I'll be a basket case for the first concert."

"Ah, but that's when you're rewarded. After the concert. All the real work is done, and then there's that adrenaline boost. As long as there's not a complete train wreck, which the audience doesn't usually notice anyway, the performance is the fun part for me."

I groaned. "Don't talk about train wrecks. I don't see how we can help it." I took a couple more sips. "That deaf viola player," I went on, "he's sure to mess up during the concert. He can't hear the other players and just goes off on his own sometimes."

To my surprise, I had discovered that Arthur Alexander—the crabby bass from the Methodist church choir—was also a violist in the chamber group. What's more, he appeared to be fairly deaf. Maybe that's why he talked so loud. Every time I said to start at a certain measure, he'd ask the people around him what I said.

"Don't worry about old Alexander. He pulls his horns in for the performance. I know he crashes around a lot during rehearsal, but he'll lay low for the real thing."

"That would be good. By the way, my schedule says there are a couple of committee meetings this week—finance and publicity."

"There's no need for you to be there, unless you want to."

"I'd like to go to a few, at least at first." I felt the wine beginning to relax me. My neck and shoulders had been in knots after the rehearsal, with me wondering if I'd done okay.

He agreed that it would be a good idea for me to go to the meetings, but not forever. We talked for a while about some of the technical aspects of conducting the pieces, then Roger asked me how I liked the program that had been chosen.

I hesitated, not knowing if he had been the one who selected it. I soft-pedaled my comments. "Well, I like all the pieces and they fit together well. But...I wish we were using the flute more."

"So you don't like the programming," he said, with an audible flatness in his voice.

Oh brother. So much for soft-pedaling. "Yes, yes, I do. I think it fits together extremely well. It'll work just great." My knee started to jiggle nervously because I didn't think the Pleyel pieces should have been included at all. They were much too easy for the group; they had just tossed them off at rehearsal.

"You sure?" he said.

"Oh, yes. Definitely." I can be such a liar.

"Great. I put it together."

Knew it!

I stroked my locket, my link to my Gram and serenity. She used to say, "Men take criticism like oil takes water." Of course, she sometimes meant my father, her son-in-law, when she talked like that. He hadn't been an absolute tyrant, just a mostly absolute one, from stories I'd heard. I had a few memories of my own, childhood experiences, when my parents took me with them and stuck me on stage.

Roger seemed a little cool when he said goodnight. I would need at least another glass to undo the knots that had returned.

Why were the male musicians I'd met lately such big babies?

Just for balance, and because I was missing him, I called Daryl right after I poured another glass of wine. I remembered this time that his show was coming up on Saturday, gave him my good wishes for it, and then unloaded all of my stuff on him. I told him about the programming for my first concert, about the contentious choir director at First Methodist, and about the argument I witnessed Sunday morning between the Nursery School director and Barry, the improbable brother of Madison Streete. I even mentioned Alexander the Great Big Bigot, who was also my Problem Violist.

"But, in general, it's a good group," I admitted. "All the members are interesting people. There's a doctor, a couple of programmers, a mail carrier, one chemist, and the rest music teachers. We'll have fun since they're all there because they love making music."

He asked me if I was making any new friends. I mentioned Maddy and Olive, then told him I even had a lead on an organist job. I started to tell him about it, but he broke me off.

"Sounds like you're settling in."

"Yep. Getting there."

"So, how long do you think you'll be there?"

He had asked me that when I left, but I didn't have any more of an answer now than I did then. The truth was, I wanted to stay here long enough to see the group grow into a full-fledged orchestra. I knew that might take several years. It would be a real accomplishment to create such a group from scratch.

"I miss you, girl," he said softly. "Wish you were still here."

"I miss you, too," I said truthfully. "Why don't you fly over after your show? Maybe you could come for my first concert."

"I don't know if I can get away."

"Don't you even want to know when the concert is?"

"Okay, but I don't have any vacation until spring break."

"Maybe my concert is during spring break." I shot back. My knee was going crazy.

"Oh. Well, is it?"

"When is spring break?" My little finger gave a sudden throb where it had been broken.

"I don't even know. I'd have to look. Listen, I need to get back to work. I still haven't finished the last piece for the show."

"Okay. Dar, I miss you."

"Miss you, too, Cress."

"Love you, Daryl," I said to dead air; he had already hung up.

Chapter 11

Impromptu: An improvisation.

Tuesday morning I had two interviews scheduled at Hopkins Heights Presbyterian Church, one with the minister, Willard Linger, and one with the pregnant organist, Sharon.

Hopkins Heights Presbyterian stood directly across the road from First United Methodist. The buildings were similar in style, handsome stone- and brick-faced edifices with flights of front steps and stained glass in the sanctuary windows. This one had a much higher bell tower, though, topped by a pointed spire roof.

I walked up the front steps and found the office down a hallway to my left. Trudy, the secretary, greeted me by name and showed me to an empty Sunday School room where Sharon was waiting for me. We sat in wooden chairs facing each other across a wooden table. There were faint crayon marks on the tabletop and I remembered Barry's rant about the tables in the Methodist church.

Sharon was a small woman with a curly cap of dark brown hair. When we shook hands, I noticed that her fingers were long for a short person. Her grip was as strong as mine. We keyboardists tend to overdevelop our hand muscles.

She explained that her blood pressure was rising and, for the health of her twins as well as herself, her doctor had ordered strict bed rest. The twins were due in five months, though they might be born early, you never knew with twins.

"The timing isn't a problem," I said. "I'll be glad to fill in however long you need me."

"Good," she said. "I also don't know how soon I'll be back after they're born. I'm taking the rest of the school year off from my teaching job."

"How much leeway do you have in what you play?"

"I pick whatever I want for prelude and postlude, but I have no say-so in the hymns, supposedly." She gave me a pointed look.

"Supposedly?"

Sharon shifted in her seat and grimaced.

"One of them is a kicker," she puffed, smiling and caressing her protruding belly. "It's really Willard's job to pick the hymns, to make sure they'll go with the sermon and the scripture readings. And he always used to do it. But lately he just hasn't. So I've been looking up the verses for the next Sunday and picking something that will go with them."

"Where do you look up the verses?" I asked.

"Pastor Willard used to use the lectionary, so that's where I look."

"What's a lectionary?" I asked.

"It's a list of scriptures for each Sunday. Most ministers use them as themes for their worship that week. I think several Protestant religions use it. It gives, like, a verse from the Old Testament and one from the New Testament and, I think, a Psalm and something else. You can pick one or two, or even use all four if you want. I don't know anyone who does that, though. Willard always used to base his sermons on the lectionary, most often either the New Testament verse or the Psalm.

"But it seems," she went on, "that he just preaches on one topic these days, 'the high places.' He's obsessed with that. We're all terribly worried about him lately." Her pleasant face showed a frown of concern. "He seems awfully depressed. And, well, strange, I guess."

Just then a soft knock sounded on the door and a large, gray-haired man shambled in. He was clean-shaven, but his hair was mussed and his clothes were rumpled.

"Trudy said I needed to meet someone?" He looked around the room, his eyes vague.

"Yes," said Sharon, suddenly overly bright. "This is Cressa, who is interviewing to sit in for me while I have the twins."

"Ah, yes, the twins," he murmured.

"Cressa, this is the Reverend Willard Linger, our main guy." Her voice was a little too loud. We shook hands and he left his limp fingers in mine just a second longer than normal, staring into my eyes with a vacant, bewildered look. Then he pivoted and walked out.

Sharon sighed with a worried frown. "He's just not himself. He didn't used to be like this."

I was at a loss as to what to say. I shrugged at her, and she shrugged back.

We arranged for me to come back in a couple of days to play an audition for Sharon, several choir members, and Willard. We settled on late Friday afternoon. That way the choir members could swing by after work.

My cell phone tweeted as soon as I got back to my Chevy. It was Neek.

"Cressa." She was breathless. "I just found a bad omen, had to warn you, you need to watch out."

"Does your omen say what I'm supposed to watch out *for*?" Sometimes I got such a kick out of that gal.

"Well…" She sounded deflated by my skepticism.

I shouldn't give her a hard time, I told myself. She really meant well. I relented. "Okay, Neek, tell me about the omen." I started up the car so the heater could get to work. My breath was clouding the windows.

"It's sandstone," she whispered. "And this piece is so soft it crumbles."

"And that means?"

"Strife. Lots of strife."

"I think you're a couple days too late on that." I related the argument I'd heard Sunday between the nursery school director and Maddy's brother, the church trustee. "There's a lot of tension in the choir at that church, too."

"How about your orchestra?"

"That's going pretty well. It's a good bunch of musicians. I'm going to have lots of fun with them." When *I* picked the music for the next concert, it would be even better.

"And how are things with you and Daryl?"

I groaned. "Don't ask. That's another piece of strife you're late on."

"That bad, huh?"

It was Tuesday, he knew, and it was cold again, but by late afternoon the snow was almost gone. Joshua hurried up the stairs and slipped into the front vestibule. No one had seen him.

The entrance was between floors. The wide stairways of beautiful gray mosaic went both up and down. At the top was a hallway and an office with the door standing open. Voices floated out of the office. He could hear the light chatter of children further down the hall on the first floor; the nursery school advertised on the sign outside, he figured. Lots of people on the upper level.

Joshua went down. At the foot of the stairs, one hallway branched to the left and one led straight ahead. He stood and scratched his itches, then made up his mind. Straight ahead it was. This led to a huge basement kitchen.

He remembered the plate of cookies that had been left in the Presbyterian church across the street. Those cookies were the last things he'd eaten that tasted good. He hadn't had much since he left the shelter a couple of days ago.

But there was no food on the counter. There were several sack lunches in the refrigerator, though. All his energy lately had gone into feeding his various habits. Food didn't seem all that necessary most of the time. Mostly, he craved heroin. But sometimes hunger pangs would strike. Like now.

He opened one of the sacks and sniffed. A strong smell of pastrami kicked him right in his salivary glands. He stuffed the bag inside his coat and crept back up the stairs to find a more comfortable place to eat.

The two women in the office were looking at something on a desk. Neither lifted her head when he stole by, into the sanctuary on the right. He looked behind. All the classroom doors that ran the length of the hallway were closed.

It was obvious, even to Joshua, being in one of the pews would make him more visible, so he decided to go to the narrow stairway at the back. He'd been up there before.

He climbed the steps and found a choir loft furnished with wonderful soft, padded pews and completely out of sight from below. There was even a space heater next to the organ. Excellent. It must be new, he thought. He hadn't expected that. The world was a gorgeous place.

It wasn't long before he was sound asleep with his tummy full for the first time in several days. Even his feet were warm.

I had my work cut out for me, since I hadn't touched an organ for many weeks. I had stopped by the Methodist church Tuesday, after my interview at Heights, and Olive had said it would be fine for me to practice on their organ. Travis was usually practicing Tuesday afternoons, she said, but I could come in any time Wednesday.

After lunch on Wednesday, I gathered up some of my old organ music and drove to the church. I gave a "yoo-hoo" to Olive from the doorway to the office.

"Just go on up," she said. "It'll be cold in there, but there's a little space heater that Travis uses when he practices. That'll help."

I knew that the cold organ would be a little difficult to play. An organ is an instrument that includes its setting. The room—in this case, the whole church sanctuary—the organ is in is as much a part of the instrument as the pipes and the console.

The temperature of the room has a huge effect on the pipes. They change pitch as they warm up and cool down, so that the pipes one played in a cold room wouldn't have the same pitch as the pipes one played in the same room heated up.

Nevertheless, the tones of the pipes wouldn't greatly bother me since I didn't have perfect pitch, and my fingers and feet would benefit from a good workout.

I climbed the narrow, winding stairway to the choir loft after switching on the lights at the bottom of the steps. As I reached the top, I was assaulted by a wave of hot odors.

"Whoa," I said out loud. I walked over to the console and looked down at the small electric heater. It was glowing bright red and grinding away, cranking out heat. I switched it off, since it seemed dangerously hot, then ran back down to the office.

When I told Olive the heater had been left on, she wanted to check the loft out, so we both trudged back up.

"I've never known Travis to forget to turn the heater off," she said as we got to the top of the stairs.

"What on earth?" Olive said. "What's that smell?"

"It smells like B.O. and dirty underwear," I answered.

Her face lit up as she spied a crumpled paper sack next to the first pew. "Aha—Melvin's lunch! You know what? I got a call from Trudy across the street a few days ago, and she says there was a vagrant in their church last Tuesday night. Their minister saw him eating something in the kitchen and kicked him out." Her voice rose as she put the pieces together. "Then, yesterday, Melvin went to get his lunch from the fridge. He brings in a whole week's worth at the beginning of the week. He counted, and one was gone. It was the one he wanted that day, too. Pastrami on rye. He was madder than I've ever seen him, and said some things a minister shouldn't say."

She smiled at this, then frowned. "He said the whole kitchen smelled bad, too. So I wonder if that same guy was camping out up here."

It certainly looked like it.

Chapter 12

Mormoroso: Murmuring (Ital.)

It was break time at my second Wednesday night choir rehearsal at Maddy's Methodist church. Olive had been sending me innuendo-laden looks and fidgeted so much on her folding chair, I was afraid she might fall off. When we were at last out by the coffee cart, she cupped her hand and gestured furiously at Maddy, whispering, "I've got a good scoop."

"What?" Maddy said, hurrying over.

"You know that vagrant that was at Hopkins Heights?" said Olive. "The one Trudy was talking about? Well, he was here last night."

"How do you know?" said Maddy.

"Tell her," she said, turning to me.

If the church secretary thought it was okay to spread this, then who was I to stand in the way? Anyway, people in the church probably ought to know about it.

"Well," I said, "I went up into the choir loft to practice for the audition at Hopkins Heights Presby, and the heater had been left on. Plus, you could smell that he had been there. Guess he's not too clean. Oh yeah, he also left the remains of the minister's lunch."

"Melvin was so mad, he kicked a pew," said Olive, her shoulders shaking at her suppressed laughter.

"I would have liked to see that!" said Maddy, agog.

"I did get sort of upset with Melvin, though," continued Olive. "He doesn't seem to be thinking straight. It seems to me that here's a person who needs ministering to, needs help. But Melvin told me to be sure and lock myself into the office, especially after the nursery school kids leave. *And*, he told me to call nine-one-one if I ever see our vagrant. He's not hurting anything or anybody—just ate Melvin's lunch."

"And used a bunch of electricity," said Maddy. "But maybe it would be best if you called the police. Do you really want to be alone in the building with him?"

"Humph," Olive snorted. "I raised three boys, I guess I could handle him. Trudy says he's not very big."

I considered what Olive was saying. "I think I agree with you, Olive," I said slowly, still thinking. "He sounds like a lost soul. But we really don't know. Is he OK mentally? Is he a drunk? Does he take drugs? If what I read about meth or those designer drugs is true, he could be dangerous."

"So you agree? You think Melvin should talk to him, too?" Olive asked.

"Wouldn't hurt," I answered. "See what he looks like, if he acts laid back or nervous or aggressive."

Maddy agreed, and Olive said she would talk to Pastor Melvin again on Thursday. Then Powell stuck his head out the rehearsal room door and summoned us back in.

The rest of choir rehearsal was a lot like the last one—the usual fun time. Ingrid, the soprano who had stormed out last Wednesday, was back, contrary to what Maddy expected. If anything was different about her, she seemed a little more soused than she had been last week. She and Powell tangled several times. Arthur, a.k.a. Alexander the Great, the opinionated bass, muttered about "purging the choir" of "certain elements" including "fags." I shuddered. Powell had to have heard him, but never once glanced his way.

Tonight, one of the tenors got the brunt of it from Powell. He was singing the wrong words since he kept getting his tongue tangled around the lyrics to "Jesus Calls Us." He kept singing "life's wild, restless sea" as "wild's life restless sea." He got up and stormed out, but it was generally thought that he would also be back.

Powell pointedly asked Ingrid and Travis to stay for a few minutes after rehearsal was over. Ingrid glared at the request and Travis frowned, but neither refused.

"Let's do Sunday's anthem one more time." Powell lifted his arms and cued Travis to begin the introduction. We got about half-way through.

Suddenly, just as Powell was banging his baton and frowning at Ingrid one more time, she stood up, staggered a bit, then regained her balance.

"I can see this was a mistake," Ingrid slurred. "The last five years have been a mistake. This time, I'm not coming back. Powell, you can go to hell. And Travis, you traitor, you might as well go with him."

Her departure left us in a stunned silence. No one went after her. I watched Travis closely and probably everyone else did, too. He kept his face on his music for a few seconds, then slowly began picking pages up off the piano rack with shaking hands. His nose and mouth looked so pinched together, I didn't see how he could breathe.

A somber group, we put our folders away without finishing the piece and filed out. Powell didn't call us back. He stood like a statue before his music stand, gazing above our heads.

Knowing I had an empty apartment to return to, and wanting to get the bad taste out of my mouth, I stopped Maddy in the parking lot and asked if she wanted to get dessert somewhere. But she said that her brother, Barry, was baby-sitting and she felt she should go relieve him.

"He's supposed to meet someone named Woody later tonight. It's all very mysterious."

"Mysterious? Why?"

"We don't know who he is, but Barry's been talking about him a lot. He says we'll meet him soon. Woody seems to be his new partner. He's been miserable and we hope he'll feel better now."

"Business partner?"

Maddy laughed easily. "No, Barry's gay. That kind of partner. Apparently, Woody hasn't quite come out yet. Barry has only fairly recently."

I thought a moment. Many of my musician friends were gay, and I recalled several whose lives were markedly changed for the better by "coming out." I also thought of a couple of them whose lives were made worse. "Maybe he'll be happier now. I hope so," I said.

"I'm hoping, too. I might take over his bad mood for him," she said, but with a light smile that contradicted her words.

"How come you're going to do that?" I hadn't seen a bad mood from Maddy. That didn't mean she didn't have them, of course, but I couldn't picture her being cranky.

"Powell said something to me tonight before rehearsal that makes me think he's gotten wind of the fact that we—meaning the committee I'm in charge of—that we're about to let him go. He was muttering about backstabbers and glaring at me when he was getting the music out."

"Oh brother. So you think the Wrath of Powell is about to descend upon you?"

She puffed out a deep breath, which hovered as an icy vapor cloud in the frigid air. "Maybe I can put myself on the prayer list." She smiled again. "Sometime when my husband, Howard, is in town you'll have to come over and meet my family. I'll call you about dinner. Maybe next week? We could do it next Monday before our chamber rehearsal."

Good. That would keep me from dwelling on the chamber practice right up until the minute before it started. Maybe it would keep me from getting quite so nervous. I gladly accepted and was starting to walk toward my car when I remembered I had left my organ audition music up in the choir loft—I'd finally gotten a chance to practice that afternoon. So I went back into the church to get it, wanting to go over some fingerings at home. I would probably practice again Thursday afternoon, then my audition was Friday.

Not bothering to turn the lights on, I navigated the narrow stairway and had no trouble finding the music on the organ bench, right where I'd left it. I gathered up the pile, stuffed everything into my music bag, relieved that I hadn't inadvertently left the heater on—wouldn't that be a bad thing to do right now!—and started down the winding steps.

"Stupid bitch!" I heard Powell say when I was halfway down. My soft-soled boots didn't make any noise, so I was sure I hadn't been heard. No one knew I was there anyway.

From the closeness of his voice, I could tell he was standing nearby, probably inside the darkened sanctuary. His voice was emphatic, but hushed.

"You can't blame her, Powell," answered Travis's soft voice. "And it's not just Ingrid. What's gotten into you? You need to calm down. You've got to stop antagonizing everyone in the—"

"And you, Trav," retorted Powell harshly. "What's the problem? I'm hearing wrong notes."

"And you'll continue to hear them. I'm human, you know. The more you—"

"That's enough, Travis!"

"I'm telling you, Powell. Leave Ingrid alone. And you can lay off—"

"Stupid bitch!"

Powell's heavy footsteps stomped off down the hallway. I stayed right where I was, barely breathing, until I heard Travis leave the sanctuary, too. Then, I made my way cautiously down the stairs, out the front door, and walked around to the rear parking lot where my car was.

The line from *The Music Man*, the one about there being trouble in River City, popped into my head. Trouble with a capital T. Several cars were still in the parking lot, which was rapidly filling up with snow. I knew one was Powell's and assumed one was Travis's. I wondered if Ingrid was still there, and if she had heard herself referred to as the "stupid bitch" by Powell. I hoped not.

But there was something—something more than the harsh words, about that whole conversation that made me very uncomfortable. Something about the tension in both of them. Undercurrents seemed to swirl beneath the surface of what they were saying.

I hummed "Seventy-Six Trombones" all the way home to cheer me up and take my mind off their petty behavior, driving through thick flurries that threatened to obstruct my vision.

Chapter 13

Doloroso: With grief, pain (Ital.)

Pastor Willard stood outside the open door of the large classroom at Hopkins Heights Presbyterian where the youth group was having their regular Wednesday night meeting. His pain was a demon that had overtaken him, fouling his mind with its fetid, hot breath.

He could hear the noisy banter as the teenagers finished their snacks and settled onto the floor in a circle to have a short worship service before beginning their meeting. Phil, the Youth Director—who was so short he looked younger than most of his charges—could be heard trying to establish order in a preliminary, half-hearted way.

The voices of the teenagers sounded excited, Willard thought. They were always eager for whatever would come next. How could they not see what a horrible place the world was? Too soon they would learn, those enthusiastic young voices would become weary, jaded. Their fresh, open faces would close in on themselves. There was nothing to look forward to, really. Nothing. Just more of the searing pain that Willard now felt in his soul almost every waking moment.

He turned away and trudged to the end of the hallway, feeling the weight of his body with every step. He was a large man—tall, not obese—but carrying the heft of middle age. His wife had loved to cook, especially to bake, and Willard had always looked forward to her creations. They always *were* creations, for she didn't like to use recipes. She used to enter her dishes in contests, and had even placed in a couple of them. They used to have friends over for dinner once a month or so. Had all of them been Wilma's friends? They had all disappeared from his life when she did.

Since her death, Willard rarely fixed anything for himself beyond the tasteless matter that came from frozen and canned containers. What was the point?

There had been such good times when Wilma was still alive. She and he had loved to go sailing with Melvin, the minister at the Methodist Church, and his wife, Carmella. Those times were dim in Willard's memory now.

Willard's feet felt heavy, hard to move. He turned around and paced slowly back to the meeting room where he could hear the voices now united softly in the Lord's Prayer.

He knew he was their earthly shepherd. His job was to guide and counsel the young. He would give it a try.

Lurching into the room, he groaned. Silence fell as all heads swiveled his way, their eyes wide and uncomprehending.

Ah, youth, thought Willard. *They can never understand anything that's just a little different than they are.*

"Children," he said. Then stopped.

Weary, so weary. So heavy laden.

"Isaiah says," he started, swelling his chest and taking on his preaching tone of voice:

> For my thoughts are not your thoughts,
> nor are your ways my ways, says the Lord.
> For as the heavens are higher than the earth,
> so are my ways higher than your ways
> and my thoughts than your thoughts.

"The high places will give us strength," he continued. "God dwells in the most high places. 'Lead me to the rock that is higher than I.'"

Abruptly, he wheeled out the door, leaving the silent room and the staring faces of the teens and adult counselors. He shuffled down the hall and up the stairs.

"My ways are higher than your ways," he mumbled, "And my thoughts than your thoughts. Higher than your ways, higher than your ways. Hopkins Heights... heights... higher..."

The words were becoming garbled in his confused mind. He needed to sleep, to stop the constant storm raging in his head, but sleep came so rarely.

"The high places," he repeated, over and over, as he stumbled up the steep stairs. He quoted from Habakkuk as he rose higher.

> God, the Lord, is my strength;
> he makes my feet like the feet of a deer,
> and makes me tread upon the heights.

Then he moved on to the sixty-first Psalm:

> You who live in the shelter of the Most High,
> who abide in the shadow....
> in the shadow...

Willard ground to a halt. He couldn't remember the rest of the verse. He wondered what he was doing there, in this high place, in the dark. He was so tired. Lumbering back down the steps, he dreaded going to his dark, empty house.

Still, he drove slowly home through the snowfall to try to find peace in the bed he and Wilma had shared for so many years.

Joshua awoke Thursday morning, confused as to where he was. That was his usual wake-up mode lately, since he didn't have a permanent place to sleep, so that wasn't surprising. Disorienting, perhaps, but not surprising. He shook his head and some of the fog cleared.

He remembered finding the room with the nice, soft couch in this same church the night before. The night before that, he slept in the choir loft where there was a heater and a padded pew. Yes, this was *that* church again. The one with the heater by the organ.

Hot tears formed in his eyes, and he swiped at them with a dirty hand. How he wished he could patch things up with his mother and move back in. The last ultimatum had sounded pretty definite, though. His mother had finally started to come out of her depression and found the courage to stand up to him, telling him to come back when he was cleaned up and had a job.

Hah! Where was he going to get a job looking like this? How was he going to get cleaned up with no home to go to? These were his thoughts when she kicked him out weeks ago, and they were still his thoughts now. Round and round. Why didn't someone help him?

He had tried to get back into the house after a couple of days but, damn, she had changed the locks. She hadn't responded to his pounding either, except to summon the cops. He had fled into the neighbor's back yard when he saw them turn the corner at the end of the block. He had lost first his father, and then his mother. How could a mother do that to her son? What had he ever done to her? Nothing. OK, he'd stolen money from her and tried to use her ATM card. Big deal.

He had gotten very clever at snatching purses and committing what he considered minor breaking and entering. He never stole anything big, just some jewelry or small electronics, stuff that was easy to carry and pawn. The people he took things from wouldn't miss them that much. They could always buy more. They weren't homeless.

He looked around the Youth Room. There sure wasn't anything in here worth taking. There was a lavatory attached to the room, which he used, then wandered into the hall.

He crept up the stairs to the entry landing and peered out the glass panes in the front doors. It was still early, barely light, and there was only one car in the unshoveled parking lot, buried under a thick layer of snow.

His skin was starting to prickle, a sign that he needed another fix soon. Joshua knew he had stuck a baggie of heroin somewhere, but couldn't think where. If he knew where he'd been, he'd retrace his steps.

Glancing to the side, he saw the sanctuary and remembered going in there last night before he found the room with the couches. Something creepy was in there, but he couldn't remember what it was. There was such a thick fog in his mind. Slowly and carefully, he mounted the wide gray stairs and peered into the gloom of the large unlit room.

Oh God! It was still there. The body, the smashed head, the red hair stuck to the floor and a huge puddle of dark blood that colored the air with its metallic stench.

Swallowing the bile that rose in his throat, Joshua clattered down the stairs, shoved open the heavy double doors, and disappeared through the drifts as fast as he could.

He knew whose body that was.

Chapter 14

Morendo: Dying away (Ital.)

hat a contrast. Thursday was a day of light and dark. Daryl's word *chiaroscuro* came to my mind. He loved to do studies in shades of gray and umber, contrasted with bright whites. Me, I loved saying the word, but I also liked the art style.

The morning, bright with new snow outside, flooded into my apartment—partly because I hadn't gotten drapes for my bedroom yet, and partly because I was sleeping in rather late. I had passed a restless night, the nasty, troubling conversation I had overheard between Powell and Travis weighing on my mind. With the daylight, it came flooding back.

My Friday audition was on my mind also. At least that was one thing I could do something about. I quickly threw on a pair of jeans and a sweater, and drove through the newly-plowed streets to First United Methodist Church to practice some more, stopping on the way at the local bakery for a bagel.

Walking into the shop brought Ingrid to mind, since I had seen her here the last time I bought breakfast. She'd said she and Travis were having problems. He stood up for her though, when Powell was so upset last night. Maybe there was some instability there. In Ingrid, that is.

What a mess! I chowed down on the bagel. It tasted okay, but was dry and doughy. I had left off the cream cheese so my fingers wouldn't need wiping before I hit the keys.

Inside the church, I stomped my wet boots, ran up the inside stairs and passed the office, waving "hi" to Olive. Then I hurried into the sanctuary to do my practicing for the audition at Hopkins Heights.

I stopped to get my bearings because it was so dark. But I was able to make out a large bundle on the floor. Blinking to adjust to the low light, I stepped closer.

Powell's smashed head lay in a congealing pool of blood, the rest of his body oddly broken and twisted. I began panicking, noticing that his face and neck were dark red, almost matching his hair, except for a purple bruise at the back of the neck.

Gulping, then breathing through my mouth to block the stench from my nostrils, I backed out of the sanctuary and staggered into the office. I was determined not to throw up.

"Olive," I croaked.

She motioned wait-a-minute and continued her phone conversation.

"No, the Nursery School Board has the Fireplace Room tonight. Doesn't the Worship Committee usually meet next week?" She paused and gave me another look. The shock must have shown on my face because she ended the conversation, dropped the phone and rushed over to me.

"What's the matter?" she said. "You're white as the snow outside."

I could only flap my hands and point, in danger of hyperventilating. Can a person hyperventilate and throw up at the same time?

We both walked back to the horror that lay at the back of the place of worship. Then Olive led me to a chair in the office while she dialed the police.

Olive, Pastor Melvin, and I had been questioned and re-questioned, but the police still wanted us all to remain in the office while they continued to search the building. Melvin told them of the vagrant, and I mentioned the evidence I had found of his stay in the choir loft. They wanted the remains of Melvin's sack lunch, but Olive had thrown it out.

It started getting chilly and Olive murmured that the furnace must be on the blink again. She fretted to the police about calling the repairman, but wasn't allowed to.

I heard a female officer speculate that since the body was lying directly under the choir loft, Powell had probably fallen over the railing—had he been pushed?

It seemed to take hours and hours for all of the various officials to examine the many aspects of Powell's death. They scattered all over the building with lights, cameras, and evidence bags while we huddled, shivering, in the increasingly cold office.

Melvin pointed out, softly but angrily, that the vagrant had probably pushed Powell to his death during the night. "Powell probably discovered him using the choir loft for a homeless shelter. The sooner he's caught, the sooner we'll be safe."

Olive said reasonably, "Why would Powell be in the choir loft last night?"

"Maybe he heard something and went to check it out."

Olive's expression told me she didn't believe a word of Melvin's suspicions.

But if the vagrant hadn't pushed Powell, then how had he gotten over the railing? Could he have fallen on his own? And how would that happen? I remembered the quiet, intense conversation I had overheard between Powell and Travis the night before. Powell had been extremely angry at Ingrid. But I had seen no signs that Powell and Travis liked each other, either. Of course, I couldn't think of anyone who actually did like Powell. Many of the choir members admired his abilities, but he wasn't a warm person, wasn't easy to like.

When the body was finally wheeled out and the photographer, medical examiner, and about twelve other people left, Olive dialed the furnace repairman and I headed for home and a long, hot bath. Even though I hadn't touched anything dirty, I felt besmirched. I scrubbed until my skin hurt.

I remembered doing the same thing when I found my Gram's body at the lake. That seemed so long ago.

Chapter 15

Al solito: As usual (Ital.)

Melvin had to admit, driving home that night, Olive was probably right. They had worked together over four years and he had learned her instincts were good, and her heart even better.

Thank you, God, that she's here to keep me on the right track when I need it.

She was not only good, she was tough. Not one bit afraid of the young man who had slept in the church the other night—and had stolen his lunch. She didn't seem to consider it a real possibility he was the person who had killed Powell...

No, no. Again, Olive was correct. He *was* a child of God. Everyone was created a child of God, all were equal in His sight. Even if the boy was a killer, he could be redeemed. Melvin felt he should try to help him. But before he turned him in, or afterward?

Was that light ever going to turn? And was the car heater ever going to start putting out heat? He cranked the knob higher on the dashboard of his very old Dodge.

Melvin's parishioners were usually law-abiding people. Of course, there was the occasional shoplifter, quite a few adulterers, and some who treated their wives and children badly. A percentage of the teenagers in any given year had brushes with the law: drugs, traffic violations, generally keeping bad company. It was a small percentage, though. Most of the kids were good kids. Most of the adults were good adults.

But this guy—the intruder—he was pretty strange. Melvin didn't know what to think of him, what to expect, and thus feared him. He hadn't had much contact with the homeless. He'd always let others work at the food pantry and the homeless shelter. Maybe he should change that.

If Olive brought the guy to him, he guessed he'd have to talk to him. But then he would call the police. Melvin smiled at the image of Olive dragging the miscreant into his office by his collar—or maybe his ear. Ah, the car was beginning to warm somewhat. This time of year you had to leave the heater all the way up. No sense turning it down until spring.

A salt truck turned onto the road in front of him. Melvin groaned and thought, *Just what my car needs, a salt bath!* He thought some unholy thoughts and turned at the next corner. A longer way home, but at least he wouldn't be behind the truck.

His brow furrowed over another recent problem. Barry. Barron Slade. How could he be Maddy Streete's brother? They were two such opposite people. Their session Monday night continued to worry Melvin. He had half expected Barry to not show up, but was pleased when he did. The poor man needed professional help—more help than Melvin could give him, in Melvin's opinion, which was what he had told Barry. There seemed to be almost borderline bipolar behavior there. To be sure, Barry had his share of problems. At least he had a steady job, and a good one, as an insurance claims adjustor.

Barry had insisted on confessing his deepest feelings to Melvin and the words gnawed at him. Barry had looked around the room nervously and said, "I'd rather die than lose him. If he leaves me and goes back to the other guy, I don't know what I'll do. I might be capable of... I don't know what."

Did that mean he could have killed Powell? Because he was referring to Powell, Melvin was sure of that. Barry hadn't named any names, but he'd told Melvin that he called his new lover Woody Woodpecker because of his red hair. How many red-haired gay men were in Minneapolis? He smiled slightly. He certainly didn't know the answer to that, but Powell was right there and so was Barry.

Should he say something to the police about Barry? Among Protestants it was understood the minister wouldn't betray a confidence unless there was a compelling reason. Legally, he was required to notify officials if he knew a crime was being contemplated, if someone might be harmed if he said nothing. Different rules for him than for Catholic priests, who maintained the sanctity of the confessional, though even that was being legally challenged these days.

But what was the proper action for him? He wasn't legally bound to say a thing, but he felt he was morally bound. Did he really think Barry had killed Powell? Was there a threat to anyone else? Powell's former—uh—companion? No, they called them partners now. The whole situation was as murky as his windshield. He had needed new wiper blades for at least a year.

Melvin heaved a huge sigh, puffing his breath out so strenuously the windshield fogged up in front of him.

Great, the inside and *the outside are opaque.*

Swiping the vapor with his gloved hand, his thoughts turned to his friend, Willard Linger.

His wife Carmella had been very close to Willard's wife Wilma. After Wilma's death, he and Carmella worked hard to include Willard, just as they had always included Willard and Wilma as a couple. But, over time, they drifted apart.

Now Melvin was hearing alarming things from Olive, via Willard's secretary, Trudy. Willard seemed to be unraveling. He'd been missing meetings and people weren't paying attention to his sermons. Much as Melvin meant to call him, he hadn't until last night. That is, he tried to call. Willard wasn't home. Melvin tried until ten o'clock, but never got him.

He remembered the one time they had taken Powell with them sailing, nearly two years ago. It hadn't been a pleasant excursion, at least, not for Melvin. Wilma's death was still very recent for Willard, plus Powell was difficult to get along with in the best of circumstances. It had been Willard's idea to invite Powell. He said he thought Powell needed some friends, maybe he would be less abrasive if he felt he were liked. He'd heard much about Powell from Melvin, who considered the choir director a thorn in his side.

Melvin flicked on his windshield wipers to clear the slush the SUV in front of him splashed onto his windshield. It smeared so he could hardly see. His windshield washer was out of fluid, naturally. The blades squealed over the glass. Well, he was almost home.

Yep, that sail had been odd, all right. Willard was trying his best to be jovial and outgoing and Powell didn't respond at all, even though he knew Willard had just lost his wife. Afterward, Powell never mentioned it, never said "Thanks" or "Let's do it again." Which was just as well, since neither Willard nor Melvin would have asked him again.

The windows in Melvin's house were lit. They welcomed him home to normalcy, warmth, and love. He breathed a sigh of contentment and he put his professional problems into their compartment for the evening, put his faint sense of guilt over a happy marriage in there too, and went in to embrace Carmella and have dinner together.

Ingrid ran to her kitchen phone. Maybe it was Travis. Hadn't come home last night again. Maybe he changed his mind. But would she take him back if he did? She swiped at her nose with a tissue before she picked up the receiver.

"Ing? Can I come over? I have *got* to show you something." Katrina, her sister. Her sister who was getting married in a week. Who was so bubbly and happy, she'd started floating instead of walking.

Ingrid suppressed a groan and said, "Sure, come on over." Would do her good to be around Katrina, maybe lift her spirits. God knows they couldn't get much lower.

Travis was acting like a huge weight was lifted from his shoulders. Kind of narrow shoulders. A mean thought, but she felt mean.

Who the hell he thinks he is? Just drop a bombshell like that.

No, not a bombshell. More of a hand grenade. Didn't kill her. Just tore pieces out. Pieces of her heart.

"Ingrid, there's something I have to tell you," Travis had started.

"Mmm?" Her favorite reality show was on. "This is getting good. Come and watch."

"Ingrid." A little louder.

Looked up alarmed. "What is it? What's happened?"

Travis took a deep breath, let it out evenly. "Okay." Sat down on the chair beside the couch, where Ingrid was. "This isn't easy for me to say. I've been wrestling with it for... well, for a long time. You know all the nights I said I was working late?"

"Yeah?" Very cautious now. A mistress? This is how the wife hears it on the soaps.

"I wasn't."

"You weren't." A mistress. For sure. Didn't let her face show anything.

"No. I was seeing someone."

"Oh, Travis." The TV droned on unheeded. An annoying background of car commercials at the moment. "You had an affair?" Might as well say it.

"Well, yeah."

"But it's over now? It's finished?" Should she hope that?

"Well..."

"Oh, baby. We'll work it out." Stretched a hand out to him. He drew his back. "No, we can't."

"Sure we can, Travis. My parents did. My Dad came home one night and—"

"Ingrid. Listen. I wasn't seeing another woman."

"You weren't?" Extremely puzzled now. Didn't he just say he had an affair?

"I was seeing another man."

Stunned silence. Absolutely stunned.

The weatherman broke in with a winter weather advisory. "Stay tuned to this channel for updates throughout the evening."

Was her heart beating? Was she breathing? Yes, she was. Stinging tears were coursing down her face.

Travis moved from the chair to the couch and put his arm around her.

She swatted it off. "Don't you touch me! Get out of here." A man? He was seeing a man?

"I was leaving anyway." He got up and took a couple of steps toward the bedroom. "I have a place to stay. I'll go pack. I'm sorry, baby. I've wanted to tell you for a long time. I thought this could work, but…"

She grabbed a hardcover book from the coffee table and heaved it at him. It missed. "Thought it would *work*?" Screaming now. "Thought *what* would work? Thought you could fool me forever? Thought you could blame me for all our problems? Is *that* what you thought would work?"

"No, that's not what I meant. I meant…I don't know. I just… I really loved you when we got married, Ingrid."

Then he turned and went to pack.

Travis had really loved her when they got married?

Must mean he doesn't anymore.

Katrina was at the door.

Ingrid opened the door and Katrina bounced in waving some papers.

"Look what just came! And they're beautiful! Just what I wanted. Aren't they cool?" She pushed the door shut and shoved a small white box under Ingrid's nose. Ingrid took it and opened the lid. Little pearls on an invisible strand nestled next to a pair of pearl stud earrings. Katrina floated around the room like a bubble from a child's wand.

"I was afraid they wouldn't get here in time," Katrina babbled on, oblivious to Ingrid's dark mood. "Our order got lost in the mail and they had to redo it—what a mess. But they made it! What do you think?"

"And these are for?" asked Ingrid.

"Oh, silly me, they're for the bridesmaids. I know I probably shouldn't show you yet, since you're getting a set, but I just had to."

Had to admit. "Yeah, really pretty. They'll look great with the dresses."

"I think so, too. That's why I ordered them." She giggled and shook herself with pure joy.

Ingrid took Katrina's hand and looked into her eyes. Such sparkle! "Look, Sis. How sure are you of Kerry?"

"Oh, Ing! I'm a thousand percent sure. He's the best! I'm marrying him, aren't I?"

"Well, yeah, but I married Travis, too."

"Are you and Travis still having trouble?" Her voice down a couple of pitches, the bubble gone out of it. Ingrid swallowed, then spoke.

"Travis moved out. Couple of days ago."

They both turned and collapsed onto the couch.

"Oh, Ing!" Katrina hugged her sister as Ingrid burst into sobs.

"Katie, he's gay," she wailed.

"Oh. My. God."

"Yeah, that's what I thought," Ingrid snuffled. Really, she'd already cried for enough hours. "He suddenly decides he's gay and he goes waltzing off to all these support groups and coming-out parties and shit. It's like a big celebration."

"And here you are."

"And here I am."

"You should have called. You should have told me."

"I was going to. I just… just hadn't done it yet. Kate, I'm so confused. How could I not know?"

"Don't ask me, Sis. I guess you two weren't getting along too good lately, right?"

"That's an understatement. One temper tantrum after another. And no sex for ages."

"You're really *so* much better off without him, you know." She gave her sister another squeeze.

Ingrid heaved a sigh. "I'm sure you're right. Just have to get used to it. It was such a shock. Never imagined."

"Oh, Sis." Katrina held her sister for a long time.

Chapter 16

Lebhaft: Lively (Ger.)

Friday morning I absolutely had to practice. My audition for the Hopkins Heights Presbyterian organist job was that afternoon, and I had lost Thursday as a practice day. Panic gripped my stomach as I headed out. Auditions—ugh!

Practice, practice, practice, I intoned as I headed for the Methodist church. Practice, the bane of my childhood, but the way, according to the old joke, you get to Carnegie Hall.

When I was a very young child, my parents dragged me along every time they went on the road. Among the three of us, someone was always practicing. They had a nightclub act, sort of a comedy-classic-music-jazz thing unique to them. Mom sang and Dad played the piano. They got gigs in Chicago, but went on the road every time one of their albums came out, usually to places like Peoria, Paducah, and Pontiac, occasionally downtown Detroit or Cincinnati.

When I entered grade school, they limited their road trips to school holidays and summer vacations; but as time went on, they were performing more on the road than at home. Then they got a venue in Las Vegas and spent much time there. It was a relief to me that I was included less and less as I got older. Maybe I wasn't as cute at eight as I was at three years old.

All the while I lived with my parents, I had a mandatory practice schedule, two hours a day, no matter what. If I did one hour one day, I did three the next. The piano in our house was near a window and I would hear the voices of children playing outside, running free, while I slaved over the keyboard, perfecting scales and exercises.

If we were on the road and the place had two pianos, they'd put me on stage doing two-handed piano pieces with Dad. Gram let up a little on the practice after they died, but not much. After all, she's the one who raised Mom to be a musician.

I swore I would never be a musician.

Did I become an engineer or a deep-sea diver? Nope, I defied my parents by choosing classical music on a stage instead of a variety act on the road. And here I was, practicing for another audition. Something I had finally grown to love—practicing, not auditioning.

My cell phone chirped. It was Neek. I put the phone on speaker, steering with my left hand.

"Yeah?" I didn't need an oracle today.

"You all right?" she asked. I guess I sounded a little short.

"I'm nervous about this audition. I didn't practice much yesterday." *I shouldn't take it out on Neek, though. She's about the best friend I have.*

"What audition? Why not?"

"Oh, where to start? The organist at the Presbyterian church is having twins, so I'm auditioning this afternoon to fill in for her while she's gone. I went in to the Methodist church to practice yesterday and, well, the choir director had fallen from the choir loft."

"And?"

"And the floor is really hard tile." I didn't want to say the word.

"So he's dead?" Her voice barely whispered through the tiny cell phone speaker. "How awful."

"Yeah."

"Looks like I'm late on this omen, too."

"Okay, I'll bite. What is it this time?"

"A fossil. A real, honest-to-God fossil."

"Which means?" Honestly, I always had to drag the portents out of her. It was like trying to make the basses keep up with the flutes in a junior high school orchestra.

"Bad news. About a dead person."

After we hung up, I wondered if she meant bad news about a person being dead, or bad news about a person that was already dead. Like maybe one of my parents.

As a child, I often had fantasies that they weren't my real parents, probably because I couldn't bear the thought that they abandoned me so easily and so frequently. I was left with Gram so much that it didn't seem unnatural, eventually, for me to move in with her for good after their fatal accident.

The memory of the shameful relief I felt when Gram told me of their deaths hit me in the stomach with a fortissimo tympani crash, as it usually did. That memory was followed by one flitting through my mind, brief as an appoggiatura, of Powell saying he knew my parents, and another of Arthur hinting that Powell knew something of their death. A new sorrow washed over me. I'd never know what it was now—unless I learned it from Arthur.

When I arrived at the Methodist church, I saw a white van in the parking lot with the name of a private hazardous cleanup company on the side. In the sanctuary, people wearing hazmat suits were cleaning up the bloodstains on the floor beneath the railing to the choir loft.

What a dismal job that must be.

I could feel even sorrier for them because, apparently, the heat was still out. Their breathing was visible in the icy sanctuary as they scrubbed.

When I got up to the choir loft, I couldn't suppress a shiver. This was the last place Powell had been alive. I peeked over the railing at the clean-up workers below and shivered again. Heights were not my favorite thing. I leaned against the railing. Gently. I didn't want it to give way on me. But I wondered how easy it had been for Powell to fall. If he fell. If a person leaned on the railing just right, he could flip over it. I turned to my task.

I pulled the stack of music from my trusty old canvas bag. The bag was at least twenty years old, tattered and gray, but it was the perfect size to carry my music.

When I stuck the sheets onto the organ's wooden music prop, the bottom sheaf fluttered to the floor. It was an organ concerto that I didn't own. I realized it had to belong to Travis. I must have grabbed it by mistake when I picked up the music in the dark, the night I had heard Travis and Powell arguing below. The concerto was several pages long and, when I picked it up with my fingers, stiff from the cold, I knocked over the heavy, black music stand that Powell used when he conducted. It fell with a clang, scattering the music Powell had left on it. Voices murmured below me, I peeked over the railing and apologized for making a racket, then righted the stand, gathered the pages, and put them back.

It was one of those big cumbersome stands with a solid back, must have weighed several pounds. I just stuck the sheets back any old way. Someone else could deal with Powell's music, not me. It sure wouldn't matter to Powell.

When I had finished some warm-up pieces, I spied Travis's Methodist hymnal on top of the console and realized I could stall a little more before grinding out my audition pieces. I thumbed through it, dislodging an index card holding neat handwritten numbers, 261 and 437. I flipped to them and found a couple of old favorites, *Lord of the Dance,* and *This Is My Song,* which is set to the stirring melody of *Finlandia* by Sibelius.

I worked all morning in the cold choir loft, finally coming down around noon to warm my fingers. The little space heater in the loft wasn't making much headway against the bitter cold. The disaster-cleaning people had left and the floor bore no traces that anything horrible had ever happened there. I sniffed, the air smelled fresh and clean.

I entered the office, and noticed Olive was wearing her coat. "The furnace man just got here ten minutes ago," she said through chattering teeth.

"No wonder it's so cold in the choir loft. Even with the heater going, I can't get it warm. I think it seems even colder, too, because I know Powell died there."

I shivered at the thought. Olive shuddered with me. "It's such a horrible way to die, don't you think?" she said.

"It would be awful, I agree, falling like that." But I could think of worse ones. For instance, being pushed. That was not a rumor I was going to start. "Have you heard anything about the nursery school board meeting last night?" I asked. I knew Ginny was going to tell the board about her breast cancer at the meeting.

"It went well," answered Ginny, coming into the office behind me. She beamed and the smile made her usually worried face relax into a soft beauty I hadn't seen before.

"The board was very supportive. They're fine with me being off for a few months to have treatment after the surgery. Of course, they know my assistant will do a good job."

"You think so?" blurted a loud voice from the hall. Barry stomped into the office. "Why would she be any better than you? Aren't you the one who trained her?"

"Barry!" said Olive. "What are you doing here?"

"I was driving by and saw the furnace company's truck. If there's a problem with the furnace, I should be called. Why didn't you call me?" He jutted his large chin out at Olive.

"It's no big deal." Olive shrugged, unfazed. "The furnace goes out at least three times every winter. I know this is your first year on Trustees, so you probably don't know that. I always just call the same people."

"That sounds like a big deal to me. It should be fixed right. You shouldn't have to put up with that."

"Barry, the furnace is so old they can't buy replacement parts for it. They do the best they can. The only permanent solution is to buy a new furnace, and the church can't afford that."

"I should at least know about the problems," he insisted.

I wondered why he was so focused on a furnace. After all, a man had died.

"I agree. And I did leave a message at your home this morning."

"You don't have my cell phone number? Oh yeah, I got a new one." Barry shrank a little as he dug in his pocket, scribbled on several business cards, then flung them onto the counter. "All my contact numbers are there, including my new cell phone," he said quietly.

"I'll call all of them next time it goes out," said Olive with a sweet smile. "Especially if it coincides with someone's death."

So that bothered Olive, too, I could tell.

Barry glared at her before he whirled to face Ginny.

"And what happened to the meeting last night?" he demanded.

"Nothing happened to it. We held it."

"Where? Not here. I came by."

Ginny looked a little startled at that. "We held it at my house because the church was so cold. We called school off today, too, but we'll resume tomorrow."

"You deliberately hid the meeting from me!" he shouted.

Ginny looked at him, puzzled. "Why would we do that?"

"You knew I wanted to come to that meeting and tell the board what the Trustees think of the nursery school being in our building."

He reached out and I was afraid for a moment that he was going to grab Ginny, but he stopped, took a deep breath, and drew his hand back.

"Barry," Olive warned, moving toward him. She was using her mother-of-boys voice.

He spun on his heels and left, clattering down the front steps and out the door.

Ginny's body sagged and she leaned on Olive's desk. "Have you talked to Melvin yet?"

"Yes, and he's in the process of calling the Trustees individually. At least three of the five have told Melvin that Barry doesn't speak for them. They may hold an emergency meeting to elect a new chairperson."

"Did I hear Barry's voice?" Melvin stuck his head in the door at the rear of the room. His office was just down the hall, behind the main office.

"Yes, he was upset about not being notified before I called the furnace company."

Melvin shook his head slowly. "Barry is going through quite a bit of turmoil right now. This death has affected him more than you know." He opened his mouth to continue speaking, but Olive shot him a warning look. He glanced at Ginny and me, then closed his mouth, frowning. "How did Barry seem?" he asked.

"I told you." Olive sounded exasperated. "He was angry. Livid even. Blew it way out of proportion. Yelled at Ginny for not telling him she'd moved the meeting to her house, and at me for not calling him about the furnace."

"But you did call him?"

Olive sighed. "Yes, I called him. He has a new cell phone number." She handed him one of Barry's cards. "Here, have one." She stuck one out toward me, too.

"What on earth would I want one for?"

"I don't know." She grinned. "But he left enough for everyone." There were several left in her hand.

"Oh well," I said as I took it. "They make good bookmarks."

Ginny took one, too. She left and I went back to the choir loft to practice just a bit more before I had to leave for my audition.

I ran over the pieces I was going to use one last time and gathered up my stack of music, then headed on over to the Presbyterian church.

Joshua stopped for a moment in the empty store, closed for the night. His pockets were full of small electronics—mostly digital cameras and memory cards that he had snatched from the cabinet after breaking its glass front. He was in the back of the store, out of sight of the large display windows in the front. He had jimmied the back door from the alley to get in. He knew there was probably an alarm that would bring the police, but he also knew he had at least ten minutes before they could possibly get there.

The clock over the counter read just ten o'clock. Maybe he could turn on one of the televisions and find out if they knew anything more about the dead guy in the church where he had spent Wednesday night. Last night he'd been sober enough to use the homeless shelter, but the need for a fix was rearing its sweet, ugly head.

He punched the power to one of the medium-sized televisions standing in ranks on the back wall. The set leapt to life. A news show was on, but they were reporting on a city council meeting. Joshua was bored with that after two minutes.

He scoured the rest of the store and looked over the other electronics to see if there was anything else small, portable, and valuable. Before he left he reached out to switch off the set he had turned on. To his astonishment, his mother's face filled the screen.

An off-screen voice which probably went with the hand holding the microphone asked, "When did you last see your son?"

"I haven't heard from him for a couple of weeks," his mother said, crying. She looked terrible. Her face was puffy and her eyes looked like they would itch.

"Do you think he's the person seen in the church where the murder took place, Mrs. Butardi?" the interviewer asked.

"Sure sounds like him," answered Joshua's mother. "He has a bad heroin problem. He's not allowed back here. Look what he does to his poor Ma." She dabbed her reddened eyes with a worn tissue, opened her mouth to say more, but was cut off by the reporter, going to the next story.

"Shit," said Joshua, switching off the power. "Sounds like they want me. Maybe for murder. Thanks a lot, Ma. At least you didn't tell them it was Dad."

He grabbed two more cameras and stole through the back door, down the alley, and into the night.

That evening, after immersing myself in a long soothing bubble bath, I curled up on my couch with a glass of wine and talked to Daryl for an hour.

"They offered me the organist job," I enthused. "I don't know why I thought they might not, no one else was in the running for the position."

"Well, you do play a mean keyboard." Daryl laughed. "I know you've soothed this savage beast many a time."

"I think it's a savage breast that gets soothed," I ventured.

"That, too," he said agreeably.

I sipped my wine, then told him about their minister at the Presbyterian church, Willard Linger, and about how he got up in the middle of my playing, wandered out, then came back just in time for the committee's vote. They had counted the decision as unanimous, even though Pastor Linger didn't actually cast a ballot.

"But that's not the most momentous thing that's happened to me lately," I added, and told him about finding Powell's body the day before.

"That makes two, counting the summer at Crescent Lake," he said. "You seem to have a knack for finding bodies. Is this a murder, too?"

I snuggled down into the soft couch cushions, enjoying the sound of Daryl's sweet baritone voice, but also shrinking from the remembered bloody sight and metallic smell.

"No one has said so, and I suppose it might be an accident, but I just don't know. It would be difficult to fall from the choir loft over that railing. It's pretty high. You'd have to fall hard against it, I think. There's a vagrant around who's been sleeping in the local churches. Maybe he pushed Powell."

Just then the television, which was running softly across the room, showed a picture of First United Methodist Church.

"Wait a sec," I told Daryl. "There's a TV story about Powell."

A brief history of Powell's life was followed by an interview with the mother of a young drug addict who was suspected of being the vagrant that had been in the Methodist church, Hopkins Heights Presbyterian, and—according to the news—several other buildings in the area.

The mom was an ordinary-looking middle-aged woman and was quietly weeping about her son's predicament and his heroin addiction, which had caused her to kick him out of the house.

I related the interview to Daryl as it unfolded and told him about finding the heater left turned on Wednesday morning.

"Olive and I are certain he spent Tuesday night on a pew in the loft. I didn't make it that far Thursday morning, so I don't know if he was up there or not Wednesday night."

We talked about Daryl's showing, which was Saturday, the next night. He said he felt fully prepared for it, finally, and described the sculpture he had just finished that afternoon. I wished him my heartfelt good luck, and sensed we were back on track as we hung up.

Chapter 17

Con Gravità: Slowly, ponderously; seriously, gravely Ital.

Pastor Willard heard what his secretary, Trudy, said at lunch time, but he just didn't see how it related to him. She said that Powell Peckham, the choir director across the street at First Methodist, fell to his death from the choir loft on Wednesday night.

Powell, *Powell*—the name sounded familiar... Oh yes, he was the one Melvin and Willard went sailing with—the one with a chip on his shoulder. Rude man. He'd sensed something fundamental was out of kilter with that man, but never did decide what it was. Whatever Powell's problem, he was determined to make the world suffer along with him.

Willard returned to his office and sat slumped at his desk for several hours. It was Friday; time to write the sermon. He wrote a half page, but it didn't make sense when he reread it. His pencil tapped on the paper—he still wrote his sermons longhand, a hold-out in the age of computers. Powell's death was crowding into his mind, peeking around the corners of his own neuroses.

Finally, Willard dropped the pencil to the desk. He went to his closet and got his coat. It was long past time to go home. It was late and everyone else was gone. Maybe he could write his sermon tomorrow.

Willard left by the front door, locking it behind him. After he got into his car, he looked up at the bell tower and sucked in a deep breath.

Powell Peckham fell to his death. Willard ran his hands through his hair. Ah, but maybe Powell's death did relate to him...

His thoughts spun and clicked into place. Powell fell from on high. *Good for Powell.*

He was well out of it. Maybe he understood about the high places. No one else seemed to.

Willard couldn't really say that he had liked Powell. No one really liked the pompous, vain, troubled man. Part of Psalm 141 occurred to him and he recited it softly.

> But my eyes are turned toward you,
> O God, my Lord;
> in you I seek refuge; do not leave me defenseless.
> Keep me from the trap that they have laid for me,
> and from the snares of evildoers.
> Let the wicked fall into their own nets,
> while I alone escape.

"But I don't want to escape," he muttered. "And *the trap that they have laid for me*—what trap is that?"

It seemed very important that Willard discover what the trap was.

He started the car and headed it home.

"High places. I know I have been in the high places. Wasn't it just a couple of nights ago?"

He had a memory of being up high and coming down again, but couldn't remember where that had been.

On Saturday, Maddy met Olive and me for lunch at the food court in the mall. Maddy said she had to be there anyway to get a new snowsuit for her youngest and, when she called Olive and me at around ten o'clock, we both agreed to meet at noon. I said I could get there early and snag a table for all of us, which was a good thing. The place was filling up rapidly when Maddy arrived with Olive. Maddy's five-year-old, Emily, only wanted French fries, but Olive cajoled her into eating three bites of hamburger. Eight-year-old Ethan, on the other hand, wanted only hamburger and no fries. He ate quickly because he knew there were video games very close. Since Maddy could see inside the narrow arcade from where we sat, she let him go.

"Now," Maddy said, sounding official, when everyone but Emily was finished eating. "I will admit I had an ulterior motive inviting you to lunch, Cressa."

I quit playing patty-cake with Emily and looked up at Maddy.

"What? What motive?"

"We're stuck tomorrow for Sunday's service. Could you lead the choir? We were supposed to do that clap-your-hands thing, but I don't think it would be appropriate."

"Good heavens, no," I agreed.

"Certainly not," Olive said with a nod as she tried to coax one more bite into Emily.

"We'll just have to pull something out of the hat," said Maddy. "What on earth is appropriate for a choir whose conductor has just been murdered? There's no section in the hymnal for that. But maybe we should sing something simple from the hymnal. Those are usually easy to do without any rehearsal."

"How about *There is a Balm in Gilead*? That's in the hymnal and gives a soothing message."

"Oh, Cressa, that would be perfect! The choir knows it, too. We just sang it a few weeks ago. So you'll lead us?"

I shrugged. "Sure. I could do that. Do you think there is a conductor's copy in with Powell's music?"

"There should be. Even when he did pieces straight from the hymnal, which wasn't that often, he always made a copy of the page and wrote his own notes on the music. His folder should be right where he left it."

"Yes," said Olive. "I noticed it in the rehearsal room on top of the piano."

"Maybe I could get that today?" I asked.

"I'll go let you into the church from here if you'd like," said Olive. "I have a set of keys."

"Good, so that's settled." Maddy breathed a sigh of relief. "At least something is going right."

Olive gave her a look of compassion. Those tilted eyes were so pretty. "Is everything all right with Barry?"

Maddy sighed. "He's seeing Pastor Melvin on Monday. I don't know what that's about, but I saw it on his calendar when I was over there this morning. Frank and I thought he was doing so well last week." She stopped to wipe Emily's oily fingers and let her down. "Stay right here," she admonished.

"I had lunch with Barry on Wednesday," Maddy continued, "and he seemed content and upbeat. Even said he had found someone new and was going to tell me who it was soon. Someone who hadn't come 'out' yet."

"And then on Sunday," said Olive, "he was exploding at Ginny about little nit-picky things that bother Vanessa and no one else."

"He should just quit the Trustee Committee," said Maddy.

"I know," answered Olive. "I've talked to Melvin about that and he's working on calling a special meeting of the committee. Maybe Monday, when Barry sees Melvin, he'll resign. Melvin's coming in special on his day off just to talk to Barry."

"Oh, I don't think Barry will ever resign." Maddy's voice trembled. "He's too stubborn for that. They'll have to vote him out. And then drag him out of the meeting, probably. I've told him to quit—it's too stressful for him, but he doesn't listen."

Maddy was close to tears and Olive reached over and patted her arm.

"Whatsa matter, Mommy?" asked Emily, running to her mother.

"Oh, sweetheart," she said, reaching down and picking up her daughter as a tear spilled out, "Mommy is just thinking sad thoughts."

"Well, don't do that," answered the child, poking her mother in the cheek with a pudgy finger, then squirming to the floor.

All of us laughed at that, instantly lightening the mood.

"All right," said Maddy, wiping her face with her paper napkin. "Now we'd better go find you a new snowsuit."

"I getting big," Emily explained to us with her hands over her head to demonstrate.

Maddy started picking up her purse and her children's mittens, hats, and other shed clothing. "I didn't ask you how your audition went," she said, turning to me.

"Thought you'd never ask." I laughed. "They gave me the job until Sharon comes back. Which might be quite a while. She wants to stay home with the twins after they're born.

"Plus, there's a wedding this coming Friday."

"Wow." Olive mock fanned herself with a napkin. "That's soon! Are you all right with that?"

"Well, the music is all picked out and I won't have any trouble with it—all stuff I've done for weddings before."

"Anybody we know?" asked Maddy, taking Emily's mittens from her so they wouldn't be lost.

"I don't," I said, "but you might. The bride is Ingrid's sister."

Maddy was stunned. "And she didn't ask Travis to play? Her own brother-in-law?"

"Apparently..." I paused.

"Yes?" Maddy and Olive gave each other a look, then both leaned in close to Cressa.

"Sharon says Travis was scheduled for it until this last week. Sharon offered to do it, but told me she'd rather not, since she's supposed to be resting now."

Maddy wondered what was going on with Ingrid and Travis. She knew they were having problems, and not having him play her sister's wedding was tantamount to a blatant public announcement. Other couples she'd known tried to keep their splitting up private as long as possible. Maddy had known both of them for several years and knew there was trouble between them lately, but still…

"Ingrid is singing, but that's something I've played before, too," I said.

"Well, that makes sense at least," Maddy said. "This means we'll miss you in the choir on Sundays."

I grinned sheepishly. "You won't miss me that much. I'm not a great vocalist."

"What did you think of their minister at Presby, Willard Linger?" asked Olive.

I paused before answering. "He's a little unusual, isn't he?"

Maddy shook her head sadly. "He hasn't been the same since his wife died. He used to be a wonderful person. Vibrant and outgoing."

Olive agreed. "Trudy worries about him, doesn't think he's going to pull out of his funk without professional help."

"And I suppose there's no way he'll get that?" asked Maddy.

"Right," Olive concurred. "It's really hard for ministers to get counseling, since they're supposed to be the counselors. Pastor Melvin has tried to talk to Pastor Willard. He says Willard is too distracted to pay attention to anything. He says it's a wonder he can get up and preach on Sundays."

"Old habits die hard, that's probably how he does it," said Maddy, scooping up Emily and heading for the video store to retrieve Ethan. "I'll see you both tomorrow."

She left as I gathered my things to go with Olive. I needed to pick up the music for Sunday. I knew that was not going to be a fun day, the first Sunday after Powell's death.

Chapter 18

Obbligato: Required, indispensable (Ital.)

I didn't think I would get so flustered. Yet, for some reason, my hand shook as I raised the baton to start conducting the Sunday morning anthem. I nodded at Travis, who was seated at the organ console, and he nodded back.

My nerves made me realize it was a momentous occasion. I was taking the place of a murdered man, using his copy of the music and his baton. Taking a deep breath, I brought the baton down, beat two empty beats, and heard the voices and the organ come in with the comforting words:

> There is a balm in Gilead to make the wounded whole;
> there is a balm in Gilead to heal the sin-sick soul.

I listened to the choir, closing my eyes to hear them better. There couldn't be any words more appropriate for today, I thought. The words to this familiar hymn, I knew, were a rather obscure reference to a healing balm that had been produced in the ancient region of Gilead and was referred to a couple of times in the book of Jeremiah.

Modern Methodists didn't necessarily know where Gilead had been, but since they had sung these words since childhood, the piece had a soothing effect. As the sweet, close harmony wafted out of the choir loft, down onto the silent congregation, it seemed I felt a collective relaxation of tension.

Pastor Melvin had announced Powell's death at the beginning of the service. There were enough people who hadn't heard about it that an audible gasp arose when he stated that Powell had been murdered.

I hated to hear that word in a church—especially about one of the members.

Much muted muttering went on during the reading of the scriptures, and even a little of it into the sermon. I was glad the anthem could break the tension and give people a chance to breathe deeply. Let the music calm them.

The choir did the anthem well. The sopranos stayed on pitch the entire time, and Powell would have been proud. Travis played a dirge-like piece for the offertory, without the choir, and soon the service was over.

I thanked the choir as they disrobed. They filed out quietly, still solemn in the wake of their leader's death.

The only sour, jarring note was the look on Arthur Alexander's face. It was smug—that was the only word for it. I tried to catch his attention, but his deafness must have kept him from hearing me calling his name.

I sure would like to talk to him about the death of my parents a little more, although it most likely had been an accident. He seemed like the kind to try and stir up trouble where none existed.

Travis lingered until I thought I was going to have to ask him to leave, as I needed to lock up the rehearsal room. Finally, he stowed his music in his file drawer, gave me a mock salute, and left.

I shook the sleeves of my robe from my arms. It was inconvenient using a regular robe for conducting, but I wasn't about to wear Powell's, which had sleeves that buttoned and stayed out of the way. It was the robe of a dead man—*ugh*. It was bad enough using his baton. I wish I'd thought to bring my own.

As I gathered up the robe to put it away, whisperings sounded right outside the choir room door, growing more urgent, then turning into angry words. Soft, but angry.

The first voice belonged to Travis. "What are you talking about?"

The second, unmistakably, was Barry's. "I'm talking about Powell. What do you think I'm talking about?"

"I think you don't know what you're saying. I also think you're an idiot."

I couldn't understand what Barry said next, but Travis's response was clear.

"I loved Powell, Barry. I was his first lover. And I think *you're* responsible for his death. Keep your hands off me!"

I heard sounds of a struggle, then footsteps departing. I waited until I heard the second set leave, then slumped onto the piano bench.

Already drained from the morning service and the job of taking a dead man's place, now I was barely able to move. Somehow, my robe got hung up, but I still had to put the music away.

I picked up Powell's folder by the spine and a piece of paper fluttered to the floor. I saw it was a small piece of paper torn from a larger one. I stooped to retrieve it, but my heart stopped when I read it.

Woody,
This is not my idea of seventh heaven. Don't think I didn't mean it when I said I would rather see you dead than with someone else. Meet me in the choir loft after rehearsal tonight.
Barry

Stunned, I sank down onto the piano bench. Just then Maddy poked her head in. I whipped the scrap of paper back into the folder.

"Hi," she said. "We still on for tomorrow night?"

"Tomorrow? Oh, yeah, dinner. Sure. I'll be there."

"How about six o'clock? Howard is home this week and Barry will be there, so we can just shoot over to chamber rehearsal and let the guys clean up dinner."

I agreed and managed a smile as Maddy left. Slowly, I opened Powell's music folder and flipped the pages until I found the paper. I stared at the stark handwritten message, knowing what I had to do, and hating it.

This must go to the police. No question about it.

I would have to give them evidence that pointed to my friend's brother as a murderer. Poor Maddy. How could I do this?

My stomach roiled, threatening to rise up as I drove out of the church parking lot. First I drove home and put the note into a sandwich bag—don't ask me why, I've just seen too many movies and TV shows where evidence was put into plastic bags. Then I drove to police headquarters and merely gave the bag to the receptionist, saying it had a bearing on Powell Peckham's murder.

But she made me wait while she phoned the detective in charge of the case. A policeman carefully transferred the note to a paper bag. His frown let me know I had done it wrong. How was I to know? They used plastic on TV.

After a few minutes, I was led into an office where two people, a man and a woman, both of them large and stern, asked me questions and recorded my answers. All I could really say was that I had found the note in Powell's music. I didn't mention the conversation I had overheard. I didn't have to, did I?

How was I going to face Maddy's family—and Barry—for dinner tomorrow night?

Chapter 19

Squillante: Ringing, tinkling; piercing (Ital.)

Daryl had been so sweet on the phone last night. At first. I called in tears, telling him about Maddy and Barry and the note, while he was on top of the world because he'd sold three major paintings at his show that day *and* had gotten a commission for a garden sculpture. I wondered what it would be like to be wealthy enough to buy one of Daryl's sculptures for my own private backyard garden. If I didn't live in an apartment, that is.

He took the time to calm me down and did make me feel a little better, but there was something in his tone. A musician can hear the false notes. It felt like he was patronizing me, treating me like a child with a little boo-boo. He still hadn't said whether or not he could make it to my first concert. He said he'd check his schedule on Monday.

Well, it was Monday.

I trudged through the silent sanctuary. This church, unlike First United Methodist, seated the choir in the front, behind the altar, with the organ console facing forward and raised up behind the choir pews. It was a very convenient arrangement, as I would be able to see the conductor without turning my head or using mirrors.

I put my music on the rack and got down to work on what I would need for the wedding and for next Sunday, which would be my first Sunday as the organist for the Presbyterians.

When I was just about finished, I looked around and Pastor Linger got my attention. I realized he must have been waving at me from the rear of the room for some time. I also realized that he probably didn't remember my name, hence the signaling.

"Yes?" I called to him.

"Could you do me a favor?" he asked.

"Of course."

"Could you play these for me?"

He lurched down the soft carpeted aisle and thrust a piece of crumpled paper into my hand. Printed on it were numbers.

What in the...? Aha, I think I know.

"Are these from the hymnal?" I asked.

He nodded and turned away, started walking, then turned back.

"I'm going away, but I'd like you to keep playing them," he said.

I agreed and reached for a hymnal as this very odd man sat on a pew at the back. What could it hurt?

The first one was number 47, "Christ, Whose Glory Fills the Skies." I hesitated.

"Do you want all the verses?" I called to him.

He nodded, then closed his eyes and leaned his head back as I started playing.

When I had finished all three verses, I turned to number 377, "I to the Hills Will Lift My Eyes."

The Presbyterians believe in giving their hymns good long names. Pastor Linger got up as I started the fourth verse and walked out, but I completed it before starting on the last number he had written.

Number 204, "Jesus Christ is Risen Today," a hymn usually reserved for the Easter season, with intricate alleluias at the end of each phrase. My fingers flew through the joyous alleluias, and I was enjoying myself in spite of my eerie non-audience. I finished playing, left my bench, and looked for the minister outside the sanctuary, thinking he had gone to listen where I couldn't see him, but he wasn't in the hallway. Where had he gone?

I went down the hallway to the office. Trudy was at her desk.

"Trudy, have you seen Pastor Linger?"

"I saw him come out of the sanctuary, but I don't think he went to his office."

She came around her desk. "We should look around. He's really bad today. I don't think he's changed clothes since Sunday."

I followed her as she went to his office and peeked in. It was empty. She said, "Let's check the parking lot and see if his car is still there."

We could see from the front door that it was.

I left Trudy to search some more inside the building, and returned to the sanctuary to gather up my music. As I left, I checked with her, but she hadn't found him in the usual places. She looked even more worried than before, on the verge of tears.

I got into my car and drove forward a few feet, then noticed a large lump on the ground beneath the bell tower.

The hairs on my neck and arms rose as I recognized the wild white hair.

A robin sang his sweet, cheerful song as I got out of my car and walked over to him. He was spread-eagled on the cement, face down, embracing the pavement with his outstretched arms, and his head looked just as flattened as Powell's had. A trickle of blood seeped out from beneath his head. The cold winter sun glinted off the puddle forming beneath what used to be Pastor Willard Linger.

Chapter 20

Straccicalando: Babbling, prattling (Ital.)

I whirled around at the sudden wail of sirens. Two police cars screamed into the parking lot and skidded to a stop, one beside me, one at the door of the church. A slight black man with a bushy mustache leaped out of the driver's seat and approached me.

"Did you make the call?" he asked.

"What? What call?" *What is he talking about? Did someone else see Pastor Linger's body?*

"We received a nine-one-one call about an intruder."

He noticed the body then and gave a start. "Who's this?" he asked.

"This is Willard Linger, the minister of this church. I think he just fell from the bell tower."

Maybe. Maybe he jumped. Maybe he dove to the accompaniment of the hymns he requested.

The policeman squatted and gave the body a cursory examination, feeling uselessly for a neck pulse, then righted himself and went back to his car to use the radio. Meanwhile, his partner stood beside the car watching me, saying nothing.

I addressed him, a tall, heavy-set, uniformed man. "How did you get here so fast? Someone already called nine-one-one from this address?"

He nodded. "Just a few minutes ago." He was heavy enough that his jowls wobbled when he nodded. I noticed that the two from the other police car had drawn their weapons and were creeping up the steps toward the front door.

"There's a secretary in the office," I yelled, picturing them shooting her when she saw them, panicked, and screamed. *It's a good thing there's no nursery school in this building, the way they're waving those guns around.*

They disappeared inside. The first policeman questioned me about Pastor Linger. Had I found the body? Had anyone been with me? He took notes as if finding dead people were an everyday thing.

Well, not quite every day. But...

"I found another body last Thursday," I blurted out.

That got his attention.

"Oh, yeah?" His raised eyebrows made even his forehead seem fleshy.

"The choir director at First, across the street," I gestured toward it. "I found him Thursday morning inside the church. He fell from the balcony."

He gave me an odd look and went back to talk on his radio. When he returned he told me I could go, but they would get a formal statement later. I thought he seemed reluctant to release me. And really, I *was* probably a pretty suspicious character, having found two dead bodies that had fallen from on high. What are the odds?

I considered walking, since it was only across the street, but ended up driving over to First to talk to Olive. If I left my car at Hopkins Heights it might be complicated getting back to it, because emergency vehicles were already blocking most of the parking lot.

Actually, I would have preferred to talk to Trudy, since it was her minister who died, but I also didn't want to hang around those skeptical, armed policemen when they didn't want me to. My hands started shaking on the steering wheel during the short car trip across the street.

Olive put her finger to her lips as I entered the office. When I raised my eyebrows, she hustled me out into the hallway.

"You shouldn't be here," she whispered. "Barry's in there with Melvin."

"I'm not here to see Barry."

She eyed me. "You aren't? Why are you here?"

"Wait. Why did you say I shouldn't be here?"

"Barry just got here—he's in a terrible state, crying. I wonder if he's finally having a mental breakdown."

"I'm about to fall apart myself."

She finally noticed my distraught state. I wasn't wringing my hands, but my fists were clenched so tight they hurt. I straightened my fingers as she asked, "What's going on with you?"

"I found another dead person." Olive was speechless, so I continued. "Willard Linger, the pastor. I think he jumped off the bell tower. Anyway, he's lying there dead, splattered on the pavement."

"Willard Linger." She stared into the distance beyond my shoulder. "Do you suppose there's a serial killer throwing people off things?"

"If there is, it couldn't be..." I stopped myself just in time.

"It couldn't be who?"

"I just don't think... it could be. Don't think there could be a serial killer, I mean," I said lamely. But what I really thought was—it couldn't be Barry. He'd been here when Willard died, right? So, even if he did kill Powell, he didn't kill Willard. Unless he came over here immediately after pushing Pastor Linger from the bell tower.

The sound of Melvin's opening office door propelled me out of the church. Olive rushed back into the office as I flew down the steps, got into my car, and roared away.

I stopped to pick up a bunch of flowers and a bottle of wine on the way to the Streete's house for dinner. Maddy greeted me at the door with a harried look on her face.

"Come on in. Barry's here already. Dinner should be ready in about twenty minutes." She disappeared into the kitchen with the bouquet and the wine and I was left in the living room by myself.

Maddy must be really distracted to run off like that and leave me standing here.

The house was an older split-level with functional beige carpeting. Their furniture was equally practical. There wasn't enough time for me to even make my way to the couch before Emily and Ethan exploded into the room. They both remembered me from our lunch at the mall and soon I was seated on the couch, my lap filled with tiny metal cars—from Ethan, and stuffed animals—from Emily. They made mad manic trips in and out of the room, bringing me their treasures, and soon I was laughing at the stack of toys spilling from my lap onto the couch and then to the floor.

"No more." I smiled. "My lap isn't big enough."

"Okay," Emily said, suddenly businesslike. She swatted all the toys onto the floor and climbed into my lap herself.

A husky, pleasant-looking man came into the room, then stopped at the sight.

"Emily," he scolded. "What are you doing?"

"It's okay, Daddy," she assured him.

I quickly agreed and, sitting with Emily piled into my lap, Ethan leaning against me, and surrounded by their toys, met Maddy's husband, Howard.

He convinced them they should put the toys away and they began slow reverse trips, laden with their possessions.

"I'm sorry," he said. "They must like you. They don't always take to strangers."

"I'm not exactly a stranger. We had lunch together."

"Ah, that's good. Maddy's told me so much about you. She says you're leaving the choir to play organ for Heights. I've been traveling the last couple of weeks and just flew in last night. Maddy says you conducted Sunday, but I missed it. Strange business about Powell."

We discussed Howard's arduous travel schedule. He told me how he sorely missed his children on the road and kept in touch with telephone calls every night.

"Maddy said Barry was here?" I ventured.

"Yes, he's in the kitchen with Mad. He's not feeling very well. And how are you holding up? We heard on the radio this afternoon that the Reverend Linger died. Maddy thought it must have been while you were at his church this morning."

"I *was* there. It was the weirdest thing. He asked me to play a list of hymns, and must have gone up to the bell tower while I played the last of them. I'm convinced he jumped." I had given it a lot of thought and concluded that he had wanted me to accompany his death. It was ghoulish, but I couldn't draw any other conclusions. "Did the radio say anything about an emergency call from the church?"

"Yes," Howard answered, "they said Linger himself placed a nine-one-one call. It must have been minutes before his death."

"Why on earth would he call nine-one-one just before he killed himself? I'm glad he did, though, because the police were there right away—practically as soon as I saw his body on the pavement."

"Sometimes people will call before committing suicide, but I hear it wasn't a suicide call. Linger said there was an intruder in the building and described a young man who had been seen there before, spending the night."

"Oh my gosh." That gave me pause. Maybe he hadn't jumped.

"That's the same guy that was in the Methodist church. He camped out in the choir loft one night." But then I remembered that Trudy searched the whole building looking for Pastor Linger. She would have found the intruder if he'd been there...

Maddy announced that dinner was ready and we took our places around their large dining room table. We made meaningless chatter and ate brisket with potatoes, onions, and carrots for a minute or so—then Barry thumped his knife and fork down on the table and raised his head.

"I want everyone here to know," he started, then hesitated.

Maddy raised her eyebrows and nodded encouragement at him. She was sitting next to Barry and put her hand over his on the table.

Barry gave Maddy a weak smile, then went on.

"I had a long talk with Pastor Melvin today. He said, and I agree, that what I have to do is get everything out into the open. I've lost a dear friend. More than that. Powell was much more than a friend to me. I'm sorry I'm so broken up." Barry paused, swallowing a sob. "Powell and I were together and he was about to go public. I was so happy for a few short weeks, then… I can't get over it. Can't believe he's gone."

He dashed a hand against the tears flowing down his cheeks, and Maddy wiped one of her own away, too. "All I hope now," Barry continued, "is that they catch the son of a bitch that did it."

Maddy glanced at her children upon his profanity. He saw and gave her a sad smile.

"Sorry. That's all I hope," he repeated.

The sound of the doorbell, although a nice soft gong, startled all of us. Howard rose to answer it. We heard male voices, then Howard reappeared, looking grim. He stopped in the doorway to the dining room and motioned for Barry, who got up and left the room with him. But when shouts came from the front, Maddy and I jumped up in alarm.

"Stay here," she ordered the children, and we both left the dining room.

I was shocked by the sight. A huge, burly policeman was handcuffing Barry behind his back and a slight female policewoman stood apart with her hand on her holster.

Emily and Ethan were peeking through the doorway with looks of horror on their little faces.

"What's going on?" demanded Maddy.

The female officer answered. "We have a warrant for the arrest of Barron Slade."

"Why?" Maddy cried.

"For the murder of Powell Peckham."

Maddy slumped into me. I caught her just before she hit the rug.

Chapter 21

Sforzando: ...with special stress, ...sudden emphasis. drawling (Ital.)

Melvin was chilled to the bone, and not because of the weather, although that wasn't helping any. After dinner at home, he left to return to the church. He'd been at the church twice in one day—on Monday, his official weekday off.

The specter of Willard's broken body wouldn't leave him alone. Even though he hadn't actually seen it, and, mercifully, the news reports didn't show it—just shots of the outside of Hopkins Heights and the same interview with a distressed Trudy, over and over and over—he was able to visualize it with a vividness that cut into his soul.

He needed to lock himself into his study and face his thoughts, something he couldn't do at home with its ease and comforts.

The car slid on an icy patch as he was slowing for a four-way stop sign. Carefully, he pumped the brakes and got the car under control, his heart slowing long after the car slipped to a stop. Melvin took a frigid breath and drove on carefully.

He hadn't taken the trouble to contact Willard these last couple of weeks and this gnawed at him. Yes, he had tried to phone, but he could have done more. He knew the man was in pain—what kind of a friend was he? What kind of a person was he? Why didn't he go over to the church, or to Willard's house?

Another thought wouldn't shut up and go away, and this one shamed him the most. He suspected Willard of killing Powell.

He knew many people thought the young homeless man had done both the killings, and Willard's phone call explicitly said the guy was there. But the thought kept popping up at odd times during the day. Was Willard crazy enough to kill someone?

A slight flurry batted against the windshield and Melvin switched the wipers on low, then twisted the heater knob to see if any more warmth could be coaxed out of the vents.

Of course, Barry was Melvin's first choice for Powell's killer. This morning's session with the troubled young man had been heart-wrenching. Barry was truly bowed down with grief. In fact, his grief seemed excessive to Melvin, a bit over the top. He hadn't been with Powell very long, after all. What if his true regret was not that Powell was dead, but that he had killed him?

Then there was Barry's accusation that Willard had molested him as a teenage boy. Did he believe Barry? He wasn't sure.

Did Barry loathe Willard enough to kill him? Melvin had his suspicions.

Much as he shivered and complained about it, he had to admit, looking at the silvery dancing flakes in the headlights, winter was the most beautiful season. Nothing could surpass the beauty of new snow. He always pictured Eden that way. Not a hot jungle, crowded with plants and, most likely, humming with insects. No, a virginal landscape covered in new-fallen snow with not a footprint or a sound, a world of pure, white silence. This didn't quite square with a naked Adam and Eve, but oh well.

Did he dare talk to Olive about his thoughts on Barry? Or his thoughts on Willard? Would that be betraying Barry's trust, the confidentiality of their talks? He frowned at the snowflakes. Yes, talking to anyone other than a professional would be breaking confidentiality.

Who could he talk to? A year or two ago that person would have been Willard, before he went off the deep end. Melvin hadn't cultivated another pastor-friend to take his place. Who ever heard of a pastor seeing a shrink?

And he couldn't have talked to Willard anyway, not after his talk with Barry.

Chapter 22

Stanco: Weary, dragging (Ital.)

The phone was ringing as I entered the apartment. I almost didn't answer it, I was so exhausted. When it turned out to be Daryl, I was glad I decided to.

He must have heard the tiredness in my voice. "What's the matter?"

"What isn't? I've just had one of the most difficult days of my life."

Clenching the phone with my shoulder, I got myself a glass of milk and a couple of cookies as I catalogued the day's events, starting with Willard Linger's death, the disastrous dinner at the Streete's, and ending with my second chamber rehearsal—a fiasco of a practice with Maddy gone and my mind only half there. Should I call her after I talked to Daryl?

"I think maybe finding Reverend Linger's dead body was my punishment for turning in the note from Barry."

"What did the note say?"

I told him what I could remember. "It was addressed to Woody and Maddy said Barry's new partner was named Woody. No one called him Woody that I know of. It was probably a pet name. I can see it, I guess. Powell was redheaded and so is Woody Woodpecker. Powell's voice was a lot better, though."

Daryl laughed—a welcome sound after the tension of the day. "That's nuts, by the way," he said.

"What is?"

"You thinking that finding the second dead man is a punishment for something. Sounds like he planned it. Sounds like suicide to me."

Sounds like you're patronizing me again. "I would think so, too, except there was a nine-one-one call." I related the details between bites of store-bought, but still pretty good, chocolate chip cookie.

"Was the kid in the church?"

I finished the cookie and fished my baton out of my music bag. After this call I needed to go over the entrances in the Sarabande again.

"The mystery vagrant? They didn't find him. I heard part of a broadcast in the car on the way home, but I'll watch the news on TV tonight. Maybe they'll have more."

Daryl and I whispered tender-sounding good-nights and I dropped the phone into the charger, not feeling all that tender. At least this time he listened to me without hanging up before I could have my say.

I spread the score out on the kitchen table so I wouldn't have to turn pages and tried to run through the tricky Sarabande movement. Would I ever be able to cue all the entrances? I did it again and again, speeding up unconsciously until the tempo was impossible.

Okay. Deep breath. No one could play it that fast, you idiot. Take a decent tempo and concentrate!

I concentrated so hard I whacked the baton on the edge of the kitchen table and broke it in half. I swore and kicked the pieces into the corner.

Then I plopped down on the kitchen floor and burst into tears. The cry felt good, though. My face still wet, I struggled up and made my way to the couch where I sat, enjoying the cathartic feeling of release my tears had brought. I flicked on the television and ignored the last half of a prime-time comedy.

The news hour came before I was able to summon the strength to get off the couch, so I stayed there.

To my horror, Barry was shown being roughly escorted into the police station. His head was lowered, but he had nothing to cover his face with, and the enterprising cameraman ducked down and got a good shot of his angry scowl. My gut clenched as I thought of Maddy watching this. Would they replay this footage over and over and would her young children see it?

The contents of the note I had turned in were also aired, read by the news anchor in such a solemn, official-sounding voice they sounded like some sort of gospel.

My God. They're trying him on television.

Chapter 23

Precentor: A director and manager of the choir

I couldn't help but ponder Barry's predicament as I went about my mundane business on Tuesday. I needed bread and laundry detergent, as well as a new baton. I drove first to the grocery store on Excelsior Boulevard.

It couldn't be Barry, could it? Barry—a multiple murderer? I shook my head and reached for the bread. Naturally, the kind I wanted was on the top shelf, and it was a tip-toe stretch to get it.

Would it really be out of character, though? What anger had exploded from him! And the note implied he would kill Powell, aka Woody. A thought skittered through my head—I wouldn't be sorry to see Barry locked up, even suffering. It was an honest emotion, followed by instant guilt that made my head prickle, and nearly buried my concern for Maddy.

I browsed the greeting card aisle and picked up a thinking-of-you card for Daryl. The verse was written in print that almost resembled handwriting. *Amazing what people can do with fancy fonts.* Thinking of fonts and handwriting led me back to the note—the one that threatened Powell/Woody—and was signed by Barry. The more I thought about it, the stranger the note seemed. It was printed in block letters, all capitals. Would Barry print, rather than write, a love note? Well, the note wasn't exactly a love note, since it threatened the loved one with death. But Barry was passionate, if nothing else, and the note was full of passion. Who printed with passion, yet used extreme care? Architects, engineers, graphic artists, and… lovers?

I paid for my purchases and headed to the office supply store to buy paper for my printer. I've always loved to browse office supply stores. I bought more post-its and colored pens than I could ever use. A display of brightly-hued index cards caught my eye and I picked up a packet.

Luckily, the music store had a baton I thought would suit me well. A baton is a very personal thing, I wanted just the right combination of lightness and balance and was lucky to find one that would work. The new one had a nice heft and was slightly longer than the one I'd had for ages, but I'd get used to it. How stupid of me to break mine! Back at my apartment, the noon news was starting on the television as I put my purchases away. The autopsy results on Powell were in.

Still photos of Hopkins Methodist, Powell Peckham, and Reverend Linger flicked by while the reporter said, "The Medical Examiner's office has determined that Peckham died of manual strangulation prior to being thrown over the railing of the choir loft at Hopkins First United Methodist Church. A connection between Powell Peckham's death and that of the Reverend Willard Linger yesterday has not been ruled out. A man by the name of Joshua Butardi is being sought for questioning. Anyone with knowledge of his whereabouts is urged to contact..."

Joshua Butardi—hmm...

A police sketch appeared on the television as the newscaster said this was the alleged church intruder and possibly the subject of Pastor Linger's nine-one-one call.

The block-printed note appeared on the screen again, the actual words blurred out, with a few choice words pulled out in a caption below. I couldn't help but flinch inside. Every re-broadcast seemed to damn me anew.

"This note, according to our sources, is what caused Barron Slade, better known as Barry, to be arrested late yesterday. He is being held in the ..."

The phone rang. It was Olive.

"Cressa, could you do us a huge favor?" she asked. "We're planning a memorial service for Powell at the church for tomorrow night. Several members of the choir got together and they want to sing 'Hymn of Promise.' Do you think you could conduct for us?"

"Um, sure, why not?" I loved the piece and knew it by heart. "Are you at the church?"

"Yes, but I'm going out for lunch, be back in an hour. You can dig the music out of Powell's file cabinet in the rehearsal room if you want."

"Sure. I'll pick it up sometime this afternoon and go over it before tomorrow night. I left some music up on the organ last Friday anyway. I need to get it for Sunday at Hopkins Heights. Does the choir want to rehearse?"

"They said they'd get here an hour early. If you're here by six, that's fine. The service is at seven."

Wednesday morning I went to Heights Presbyterian to practice new organ pieces for my first Sunday there, since the songs I picked out before wouldn't be appropriate now. I asked Trudy who was preaching and what sort of service was planned, in light of Pastor Linger's death.

"We're still trying to figure that out," she said. "I know First is having a memorial for Powell tonight, right?"

"Yes. I'm leading the choir, too. I don't know what they're going to do for a director on Sunday, since I need to be here. I did get one piece of good news from Maddy this morning. They've released her brother after the family raised bail for him. He has to stay in town, though." I didn't mention that although Maddy spoke to me, she made it clear I was not her favorite person right now.

"Not a good week for the churches of Hopkins, is it?" said Trudy.

A rhetorical question, and I didn't answer. I just made a face and went into the sanctuary to practice. The list of hymns Willard had given me just before his death poked out of the hymnal I had taken with me when I left on Monday. I plucked it out, wondering if I'd ever be able to play those three again without thinking of him. I laid the paper aside and warmed up on some simple hymns. Sharon, the pregnant organist, had called and told me that the choir was planning on singing to guitar accompaniment for the anthem for the Sunday morning service, so I wouldn't be playing that.

I needed to come up with the hymns and an organ offertory, though, so I reached into my bag, pulled out a pile of music, and thumbed through my collections. I toyed briefly with a Bach Prelude, in C, number 545, that I had worked up a couple of years ago, but rejected it for my all-time favorite piece of music, Bach's "Jesu, Joy of Man's Desiring." It came back to my fingers easily enough, but my sore heart wasn't in what I was doing.

Neither Trudy nor Sharon had given me any guidance about hymns. Trudy had said it would be up to me to decide which ones to use for the service. When I was satisfied that I could pull the Bach off, I gathered my things together and stuffed them into my trusty old satchel. Something crinkled as the music went into my bag. I reached down to the bottom and pulled out a little plastic baggie with brown powder in the bottom.

For a moment I puzzled over it, then decided I must have shoved it into my bag that dark night in the Methodist church when I overheard Travis and Powell arguing. When I held it up to the light it looked like drugs, which was likely, with the druggie vagrant that had camped out there. It also looked like something the police should have.

Or should they? It had to have been in the choir loft shortly before Powell was thrown from there. This pointed to another's guilt—it just might possibly clear Barry. Did I want that? I swallowed the shameful thought and headed up the aisle. Of course I wanted to clear Barry. My personal dislike didn't mean he killed someone. Even if he did, this evidence had to be looked at. I was done here anyway, and waved goodbye to Trudy as I rushed out of the church.

Before my courage could fail me, I drove straight to the police station. I had had bad experiences turning in evidence, even before the "Barry" note. The sergeant who took the baggie was annoyed that I was touching it. He asked—accusingly, I thought—how long I'd had the baggie and I tried to explain that I had just found it.

He took my fingerprints. "For elimination," he said, then dismissed me.

The service for Powell was beautiful. The altar area of the Methodist church overflowed with flowers. Their scents mixed heavily and made singing hard for some of the more allergic of the choir members. They sang the Natalie Sleeth song as well as I'd ever heard them sing, though.

The only jarring note was the conspicuous absence of Arthur Alexander, the outspoken bass. I was sure he was making a personal statement by not singing today. No one mentioned Alexander the Great. We had enough basses and his voice wasn't missed. The words spread out over the gathering and rained comfort on them. The last verse was especially fitting for the sad occasion:

In the bulb there is a flower; in the seed, an apple tree;
    in cocoons, a hidden promise: butterflies will soon be free!
In the cold and snow of winter there's a spring that waits to be,
    unrevealed until its season, something God alone can see.

There's a song in every silence, seeking word and melody;
    there's a dawn in every darkness, bringing hope to you and me.
From the past will come the future; what it holds, a mystery,
    unrevealed until its season, something God alone can see.

In our end is our beginning; in our time, infinity;
    in our doubt there is believing; in our life, eternity.
In our death, a resurrection; at the last, a victory,
    unrevealed until its season, something God alone can see.

Ingrid's voice soared pure and light and true, and Travis's fingers found each note with a caressing touch. You'd never know there was discord between them. When we finished, the mourners gave us a moment of appreciative silence, more valuable than applause, and much more appropriate.

After the ceremony, Olive caught me in the choir room as I was removing my robe.

"Nice job, Cressa," she said. "Thank you so much for doing this."

"No problem. But what are you going to do for a choir director on Sunday?" I stuck my robe onto a hanger. "I've got to be at Heights."

"Ordinarily I would ask Maddy, but now, with Barry's problems… At least he's not still in jail."

"I'm glad he's been released."

"Yes, the bail was lowered." She leaned close and whispered, "I think Melvin talked to them, told them he didn't think Barry would try to run away."

"That's great! And I'm so relieved for Maddy. I wonder how she's doing. Have you seen her?" I asked. She hadn't been at Powell's service.

"I talked to her on the phone today. She's not doing well. Maybe you should stop by and see her. I have to stay here another couple of hours or I'd drop by."

Olive left and I stood still for a moment hoping Maddy's attitude toward me would soften with Barry's release.

I knew I should go see Maddy.

Chapter 24

Di Nuovo: Anew; over again. (Ital.)

Ingrid walked directly to her car after the service for Powell, eyes straight ahead. *Don't want to talk to Travis.* He might catch her eye, want to talk. Sanity depends on staying away from him, not thinking about him. This is how she would deal with the whole mess. Don't think about him, don't talk to him. *Seems to be working.*

Stop and get take-out on the way home, and eat it in front of the TV. *Tomorrow I'll make a tuna hot dish. Pretend I'm just a carefree single gal. Enjoying life. Travis hates tuna hot dish.*

The television rolled on to the news, but before she could switch the channel, it showed the footage—again—of Barry's arrest. There he was in handcuffs. *Must feel awful to know pictures of you being handcuffed are all over town.* She'd always liked Barry—the only gay guy she knew, really. Until she found out that Travis was gay...

This broadcast seemed different. *Oh, new news! Omigosh, they let him loose. Picked him up again. For questioning. Got a tip. What were they saying about the old Presbyterian guy? Was he gay, too?*

Wait a minute! Whoa! Maybe Barry and Travis...? Haven't thought about who Travis was seeing. He didn't say. Could be Barry, right?

They're showing the note again. Why do they show the same stuff, over and over? Guess that note means Powell was gay, too. Note was written with block letters. Block letters. Very neat. That was Travis's style. What in the hell did that mean? Travis wrote the note? Barry tried to make it look like Travis wrote it?

Most likely person to kill Powell would be Arthur Alexander, old Alexander the Great. Arthur hates me and Travis, I know. Everybody knows Trav prints the hymn list out in block letters every Sunday.

Maybe that old Arthur guy framed Travis? No, it was Barry who was framed. But Arthur doesn't like Barry any better.

What a mess!

Hold on. Remember. Don't think about Travis. Don't reach for the whiskey. Turn off the TV. Make a quick phone call. No not your cell phone. From a phone booth. There's still one at the quick mart. Tell the cops they should look at Arthur. A quick walk to the corner, then back home.

Katrina left all these bride magazines—better look at them. That's better.

The same broadcast caught Pastor Melvin's attention. He felt the weight descend, felt his eyebrows pinch together and his stomach knot. Although Carmella hardly ever watched TV, Melvin usually tried to catch the news, but hadn't been home the last two evenings. He'd been at community outreach programs, representing the Methodist church in two back-to-back meetings.

He watched the footage of Barry trying to turn his face away from the camera. Melvin had betrayed Barry's trust; he had talked to the police about Pastor Willard molesting Barry years ago when Barry had attended the Presbyterian church. But it looked like Barry might have killed two people—Melvin couldn't risk not saying anything. He was relieved they weren't saying who gave them the tip.

He leaned toward the set as a blurred image of a threatening note aired. Underneath, the caption said, "Rather see you dead than with someone else."

Wow! Pretty damning evidence. Melvin had known that Barry was seeing Powell. If only Barry had never met Powell. If he hadn't become a Methodist, he probably wouldn't have. His experience with Willard guaranteed a change in churches, though.

Barry had been distraught over Powell's reluctance to go public with their relationship. He'd told Melvin about Powell being first eager, then reluctant, to share their news. Powell told Barry he felt it might jeopardize his choir-conducting role at the Methodist church. While it was just a part-time job—his main means of support was his job as an insurance adjustor—the position fed his ego, and he loved it.

Barry, in his astute way, had known all of this and was willing to keep it a secret—except for his talks with Melvin. But Powell had been talking about going back to his first partner. That possibility ate at Barry; maybe it was what finally sent him over the edge?

Melvin felt relief that Barry was once again behind bars, but he himself was not off the hook. He was squirming on the end of that hook, feeling its barbs piercing his soul. A two-pronged hook that contained the horns of his dilemma. He'd had to either betray Barry's trust or risk another death.

Who knew why Barry had flipped or how far he would go? What made people go on killing sprees? And what made them stop? Melvin had felt there was a chance, however slim, of more deaths, and those would be on Melvin's own head.

Or was this merely rationalization on his part?

His face reddened in a flood of shame. He had given the police information that Barry gave him in confidence. The only justification for that would be if he strongly felt Barry was a future threat—some kind of serial killer. Of course he wasn't… was he? Should Melvin have gone to the police? What kind of a person was he?

Melvin squeezed his eyes shut and prayed. He asked to be able to feel sorrow for Barry and his family. He asked forgiveness for betraying Barry, especially if Barry was not the killer.

An answer of sorts was sent to Melvin when it occurred to him that turning Barry in was a way to help him. Melvin truly believed it was probable that Barry had killed Willard. Confessing this would be the best thing for Barry to do.

Barry was still being held. He would visit him tomorrow, if he was able to get in. He would see if there was some way he could comfort Barry. Maybe he could talk him into confessing.

He hoped no one had told Barry who the tip was from. They wouldn't, would they?

Chapter 25

Con Amarezza: Bitterly; mournfully, grievingly. (Ital.)

Maddy simply couldn't believe the direction her life had taken in the last few days. On Monday morning she was a contented wife, married to a handsome, steady guy, and mother of two adorable and precocious children. She was blessed with talent, an interesting musical hobby, and she had a couple of wonderful brothers. Her older brother, while sometimes angry and confused, was basically a good person. That one was Barry, and now...

Barry had never hurt anyone in his life. When she was a child, he had treated her like a princess. He adored his little sister and never teased her. But when he was in the eighth grade, things changed. He became moody and withdrawn, and by the time he was in high school, he no longer had any time for his little sis. She couldn't help adoring him, though. To Maddy, he'd always be her wonderful big brother.

When Cressa had called earlier, her first reaction was to tell her not to come over, but she quickly thought better of it. She realized that she desperately needed someone to talk to about Barry's two arrests. What a nightmare!

Ethan was scheduled for a play date after school, the other mother picking him up, and she sent Emily next door where there was an absolutely fascinating new litter of kittens and a very kind grandmotherly sort who never tired of seeing Em. So when Cressa came to the front door, the house was quiet.

"The last time I was here," she said, "it was Grand Central Station. And I was buried with teddy bears."

Maddy gave a weak smile, the best she could manage. "Would you like something to drink?" she asked.

Cressa accepted a glass of iced tea and they settled at Maddy's kitchen table.

"What am I going to do, Cressa?" Maddy asked. She didn't know if Cressa would have anything constructive to say, but she could try.

Cressa said, "I have one piece of good news. I don't know if Barry was charged with both Powell's and Willard's deaths."

"Not officially. Yet. It looks like they probably will, though." Maddy stirred sugar into her tea, clinking her spoon against the glass.

"Well, they might not be able to. I found a baggie of drugs in my music bag. I must have accidently picked it up and shoved it in there as I was packing up a pile of sheet music after I had finished practicing in the choir loft at the Methodist church. Willard called the police just before he died and said an intruder was in his church.

"It could be that the same intruder killed them both—and maybe he was the one who left the drugs in the choir loft. Maybe Powell discovered him in the loft and the intruder killed him, leaving his drugs behind in a panic? I gave the baggie to the police yesterday, so maybe we'll know something more soon."

A smidgen of hope formed. "Is that proof enough for them?"

"Well, not proof—the police wouldn't even tell me if it was drugs in the bag or not. But if there was an intruder in the choir loft, it could point at the possibility of someone besides Barry being the… you know. Killer."

Maddy's face revealed her doubts.

"I know I'm not the police," Cressa quickly added. "But—"

"You don't really know Barry." Maddy slammed her glass down on the table and jumped up. "He wouldn't have done anything like this," she said, pacing the kitchen floor. "The only times you've seen him, he was going after Ginny Dahlberg."

"Well, at dinner here that night, he was—"

"Yeah. *That* night." Maddy whirled and stopped, leaning on the counter. "It was only three days ago, but it seems like ages. The night Powell was killed, Barry was here. He baby-sat that night. He couldn't have… he just couldn't have…"

"Yes, I remember you saying he was going to baby-sit. But didn't he leave to go meet someone after that?"

Maddy narrowed her eyes at Cressa. Whose side was she on?

"Well, if he doesn't have an alibi," Cressa stammered, "the police may not be able to rule him out yet."

"Barry says he was supposed to meet Powell, but he didn't go. He says Powell called the house—probably during the choir break—and told Barry not to come because he had to see a couple of people after rehearsal."

"That's right. I remember that! He asked Travis and Ingrid to both stay and talk with him. But…" Cressa paused.

"Yes?" asked Maddy.

"Nothing, I guess. What time did Barry leave here?"

"He stayed and we watched a movie. He probably left around midnight."

"I wonder if that would clear him." Cressa seemed distracted.

"What are you saying? You think Barry killed Powell?"

"No, no, of course not."

Maddy stared at Cressa, wondering how much she really knew about her. How could she think Maddy's brother was a murderer? "Howard and I both told the investigators he was here," she said. "But Cressa, that note they're showing on television is driving me crazy. It just doesn't sound at all like Barry. He insists he didn't write it."

Cressa choked slightly on her tea and paused a moment. "And it was printed. I thought that was strange, to print a note to a lover. Does Barry usually print?"

"Never. He scribbles. Hardly anyone can read his handwriting. I don't think he wrote that note to Woody—that was Powell's nickname, by the way. He told me that just this morning."

"He did? Well, that's not good. I wonder how many people knew that before the funeral?" Cressa asked.

"Nobody I know of. I didn't even know who Woody was until I saw that note on television."

"Maybe Barry didn't write it. But then, someone else would have had to know that nickname for Powell, right?"

"I don't know. I suppose so." Maddy sagged into her chair and the tears started trickling down her face. "I'm tired. I can't think any more. I don't know what anything means. I just want Barry back…" Maddy froze. Realization dawned. "What did you say?"

"When?"

"Just a minute ago. You said the note was printed. They're not showing the actual note on TV, just the words it contained. Did you see it?"

Cressa sputtered some iced tea onto the table.

"Well, did you?"

Cressa took a deep, shaky breath, wiping up her spill. "I'm the one who found it."

"And you gave it to the police as evidence that Barry killed Powell? Then you've given them all the evidence they have so far."

"It doesn't prove anything, Maddy. I *had* to give it to them. What would you do?"

"I might just fire the new conductor of the chamber ensemble. *You* might be the murderer."

Chapter 26

Inquieto: Unrestful, uneasy (Ital.)

Joshua hated spending nights in the shelter. It was more comfortable than his usual haunts, but he never slept well. Of course, he had to be clean to be here. He left his cot in the communal sleeping room as soon as he woke up Thursday morning. He went to the counter in the dining room to get a cup of coffee. Not what he really wanted, but maybe that would come later.

The television, as usual, was playing to itself. No one was paying attention. The sound was turned down so soft it could only be heard from three feet away, which was where Joshua was sitting, drinking bad coffee and eating cold toast, when he heard his name coming from the box. He whipped his head around to the screen. The picture from his high school yearbook, sophomore year, was being displayed and some old fart was asking "anyone" to turn him in to "the authorities."

It was that damn killing in the church. He looked around furtively. Nobody else had seen the broadcast. The picture didn't look much like him today, two years later, anyway. Maybe no one would be able to make the connection.

Then Joshua froze. He remembered that he had signed into the shelter under his own name, Joshua Butardi, last night. He grabbed a second piece of toast, stuck a lid onto his Styrofoam cup of coffee and fled.

Before, they had wanted him for questioning, but now it sounded like they really *wanted* him. He supposed he'd been a wanted man before, what with the petty thefts and the heroin. But no one looked for him too hard for *that* stuff.

Powell being dead was a different thing—a whole other game. Sure, he hated Powell... but did he want him dead? Hell, he didn't even know for sure if he had or hadn't killed him. The only vivid memory he had of that night was Powell's body, his head lying in a pool of blood.

Way too vivid.

It stayed with him, even through the drug haze.

Powell had walked out on him and Ma the year that picture on TV was taken. And then his mother had fallen apart, and Josh had fallen through the cracks. Or into the crack, he'd done crack before finding heroin. No one had been there for him.

One day he had what he thought were two normal parents. The next, he had none. Dad told Ma he was gay and left. Ma checked out mentally. Even though she was at home she wasn't there for him. Josh wasn't allowed to talk about his dad any more, and when Powell changed his last name, it was like he'd never been Josh's father.

Ma stumbled around in the morning and got Josh off to school, then went to work. Some mornings she didn't say a word. Some mornings she cried. Josh tried to comfort her, but she shut him out, and there was no one to comfort Josh. No one for either of them, Josh realized, looking back on it now.

After school, Josh usually came home and watched television until his mother got there. Sometimes she fixed dinner, but sometimes she shut herself in her bedroom and Josh had to find himself something to eat. There didn't seem to be much point in going to school. He stayed home a few days, but the empty house was boring. Ma stayed home in bed some days, too, and that was depressing.

So he started hanging out with the dropouts. Pot helped some, and he stuck to that for a long time. Then, his junior year, when he realized he wasn't going to pass any of his subjects, he joined the dropouts for real, and moved on to real drugs.

The cops came around asking his mother about him one too many times. He never kept the stolen stuff at home, but she got tired of seeing cops at the door, so she kicked him out. That was a year ago. Or maybe two. He'd lost track of how long ago it was…

After his dad first moved out, he called Josh once a week, then backed off to once a month. They never had anything to talk about. Josh wasn't interested in Powell's new life and didn't want to tell Powell how bad things were going at home. The calls became less and less frequent, then stopped altogether.

The day he saw Powell dead, he hadn't heard from him for a long, long time. But even if it had been ten years, he would still know his own father. And the feeling he had when he saw him dead still cut like a knife, right through the haze.

There weren't enough drugs in the world to erase that sick, gut-wrenching feeling.

Chapter 27

Sempre: Always; throughout. Continue the previous markings throughout the rest of the passage (Ital.)

I was practicing in the afternoon on Thursday at the Methodist church. Travis had used the organ at First all morning. I couldn't get to it until after three o'clock. The sanctuary at Hopkins Heights Presbyterian was being decorated for the Friday afternoon wedding, so I didn't want to use their organ right then. But I did want to prepare for the wedding rehearsal that night. Plus, Sunday would be my first worship service at Heights. The thought of it made me shudder.

Although I was happy to play the wedding and sure could use the extra money—especially since I was on the verge of losing my conducting job—I was very glad I wasn't the bride. The atmosphere in that place was beyond gloomy. A last-minute substitute minister was performing the wedding, and Trudy had told me a lay speaker was doing the service on Sunday.

Maddy's unreasonableness steamed me when I replayed the scene in her kitchen in my head. All night it had been on a continuous loop, repeating over and over—her saying she wanted to fire me, and then accusing me of the murder that her brother had been arrested for. *The nerve!*

In my mental replay, where I was virtuously right about everything, I told Maddy off. "You can't fire me because I just quit. Your little chamber group can dissolve for all I care." Then, I imagined her looking at me in stunned silence, apologizing, and maybe groveling at my feet, begging me to return.

Practicing my music made the loop stop, at least momentarily. I put in a productive three hours, then scooped everything off the bench into my canvas bag, just like the time I'd scooped up the drug baggie, and made my way down the narrow stairs from the choir loft. I glanced at the spot on the tile where Powell had died. I'd probably do it every time I passed by.

Olive was long gone and the office was locked up and dark, but light and voices were coming from a room down the hall. Curious, I stole up to the doorway and peeked in. Ginny, standing before a couple rows of people seated on folding chairs, immediately saw me, smiled, and invited me in. I took a chair at the end of the row closest the door, feeling it would be rude to ignore her invitation, but not wanting to really intrude on what was obviously the nursery school board meeting.

Ginny said, "The reason I called this special meeting is to announce that we've gotten some good news. This will be short because Worship Committee has this room in about a half an hour. Since I am starting my treatment soon and Nicole will be taking over for a while, I initially called this extra meeting so I could say good-bye, for now, and good luck to each of you in person."

She paused and sipped from a bottle of water on the table beside her. "But, as it turns out, there's another special reason for getting together tonight." Ginny glanced at Pastor Melvin, seated on the front row. He rose with a piece of paper in his hand and faced the group.

Early Thursday, Melvin awoke with a sense of foreboding. Late Wednesday, he heard from Maddy that her brother, Barry, had asked to see him in jail. The appointment was for ten o'clock this morning, and the day seemed to drag terribly until Melvin needed to leave at nine-thirty. On the way, he prayed for strength to deal with Barry one more time and, maybe more to the point, for the ability to feel compassion for him. The interview was a pleasant surprise, though. They faced each other the short way across a long table, a guard standing nearby at the door.

"Pastor," Barry's voice was hoarse. Had he been crying? "I'd like to get a message to Ginny Dahlberg. Could you do that for me?"

"Of course, Barry." But Melvin was wary, knowing the animosity that sparked between the two of them.

Barry must have seen consternation on Melvin's face, because he hurried to reassure him. "I want to make amends, Pastor. I've been sitting here brooding, nothing else to do, and I think I've figured out what's the Big Stuff and what's the Small Stuff, at least in part. This crusade I've been carrying out against the nursery school is Small Stuff. At least compared to what I'm facing."

He clutched his hands together and stared at them. Then his eyes rose to meet Pastor Melvin's. "Can I dictate something for you to read at their next meeting? Maddy told me Ginny announced to the board that she has breast cancer. I feel like such a scumbag for harassing her when she's dealing with cancer. That's Big Stuff."

"Barry, I couldn't have said it better myself. Your predicament and Ginny's health are, indeed, the big stuff." He was pleased, relieved, that Barry had come to his senses. But why did he have to be jailed for murder to make that happen? *God have mercy*, he prayed to himself.

"And, by the way, I didn't kill Powell. I couldn't have, Pastor. I might have wanted to kill Willard Linger, but not Powell. He was the world to me. With him gone, it's like one of my arms is missing."

Barry's voice broke and he sounded genuine, but Melvin knew that it was possible he was protesting his innocence for Melvin's benefit. He couldn't blame him in his present situation, after all.

"You say you might have wanted to kill Willard Linger, Barry?"

"Years ago I wanted him dead, even thought about how I would kill him a couple of times." Melvin saw his fists clench at his sides. "But that was a long time ago. If I were to kill him, it would have been then, not now."

Pastor Melvin had brought his briefcase and proceeded to get paper and pen out. "Wouldn't you rather write your message to Ginny and the nursery school committee yourself?" he asked.

Barry held his hand out and looked at it. "I think I can. I was shaking so much yesterday I could barely hold a cup. I think I feel better just because I'm doing this."

He grasped the pen, stared at the pad of paper, then wrote for several minutes. Both men, Melvin was sure, felt the lifting of a weight as they embraced and Barry was led back through the heavy metal door.

Now Melvin stood before the Nursery Board, beaming, and began to read:

> I'd like to apologize for my recent behavior. I realize I've been unfair to the nursery school and too hard on Ms. Dahlberg. Pastor Melvin made me realize that the Trustees are overwhelmingly in favor of continuing to house your school in our building. Please accept my apologies for any hardship you might have experienced. And I personally wish Ms. Dahlberg well with her treatments.

"It's signed Barron Slade," said Melvin.

A moment of silence followed. Then, the six board members broke out in grins and applause.

"I assure you," Melvin interjected, "I had nothing to do with the wording of this. Or even the subject. It came to Barry that this was something he needed to do."

"Pastor," said Ginny. "Please be sure and tell Barry his apology is appreciated." Then Ginny held up a couple of strips of leather. "Nicole?" she said. "Would you come up here please?"

A petite young woman in jeans bounced up to stand beside Ginny facing the group.

"I hereby give these over to you," said Ginny. "The reins." She handed the leather straps to Nicole and the group again smiled and clapped. "That's all I have. I want to wish you all the best in my absence. I won't be far, though, and don't hesitate to call. If I can't talk right then, I won't. But I'm going to lick this."

They all rose and hugged both Nicole and Ginny as they filed out.

I had no idea why Ginny wanted me there, but she soon answered my unspoken question.

"Cressa," she said when all but Melvin had left. "I know you've seen Barry at his worst. It's nice you got to see the good side of him tonight. He really can be a dear when he wants to be. He's kind of up and down, you know. In fact, he's made many large contributions to the school."

"May I see the letter?" she asked Melvin.

He handed it to her.

Maybe I'd have to reconsider my opinion of Barry. "I appreciate it, Ginny," I said. "That's awfully nice of you to have that attitude."

Ginny scanned the note and handed it back to Melvin.

An idea occurred to me and I turned to Melvin. "May I look at it, too?"

"Sure."

He handed me the paper and I studied it. Barry's handwriting was, as Maddy had said, a scrawl. Almost illegible.

"How did you read this?" I asked.

Melvin smiled. "I looked at it beforehand and figured it out. And I may have gotten some of the words wrong, but I'm sure I read the spirit correctly."

"Almost sounds like he's going through a twelve-step program," I said. "Like he's on the step where he has to ask people to forgive him."

"I'm just very relieved he decided to do this formally," said Ginny. "It's a tremendous weight off my shoulders. I feel good, now, about leaving the school for my treatment. I won't have to worry about Nicole facing his hostility.

"By the way, do you know anything about this arrest business? I guess he's still in jail?"

"Yes, I saw him there this morning," said Melvin. "He asked to see me so he could write this note and have me take it to the Board."

"How's Maddy holding up?" I asked.

"I called her and read Barry's note just before I came here," said Melvin. "She's obviously quite upset."

"I'm going to call her tonight," said Ginny.

I decided to do better than call her. I dropped by the Streete house on my way home from the church to face Maddy once more.

My reception wasn't as chilly as I'd expected. Maddy looked like hell. I didn't think her hair had seen a brush that day. Or the day before. She turned her back to me, and I followed her to the kitchen where she poured iced tea for both of us. I was getting used to this local habit of having cold tea all year long.

Maddy and I sipped our tea while Howard got the kids ready for bed. We both ignored the dinner dishes waiting on the countertop. This would only be a quick visit, I told her, as I had to get to Heights for the wedding rehearsal.

"I just wanted to tell you about the Nursery Board meeting. Ginny invited me and I heard Melvin read an apology from Barry," I said. "It was a wonderful thing for him to do. Do you know about him doing that?"

"Yes, Barry had me get in touch with Melvin. He specifically wanted to give his apology to him."

"I'm so glad he did it."

"It's never been easy being Barry's sister. But it's usually been easier than this. I'm sorry I blew up at you yesterday. I know you had to turn the note in. I just wish you hadn't found it."

"Me, too."

She gave a big sigh and swirled more sugar into her tea, staring at the clinking ice cubes. Ethan and Emily ran into the kitchen and gave both of us toothpaste-flavored kisses, then ran off, leaving the aura of fresh-scrubbed kid behind.

"What do you think?" Maddy asked. "Do you think the guy sleeping in the churches killed Powell?"

"Who knows? I can't even figure out why Willard wanted us to think the kid—his last name is Butardi—had something to do with his own death. That's what the news said. Trudy tells me Pastor Willard was so confused in his last days that a person couldn't read anything into what he did, said, or even wrote. She said his last few sermons didn't make any sense."

"I'm not going to be able to sleep tonight, knowing Barry's in jail again. And for two murders." Maddy looked at me as tears spilled from her reddened eyes. "He keeps denying having written that threatening note. And they keep showing it on TV. Over and over and over."

I gulped and changed the subject. I didn't want to bring that up again.

"Do you know what the next step is for him? Legally, I mean," I asked.

"No, we're meeting with the lawyer next Monday. I don't see why anything should change by then, though."

I didn't see why either.

Chapter 28

Con Abbandono: Yielding wholly to emotion; with a burst of passion; carried away by feeling (Ital.)

Ingrid couldn't shake her depression. At least she was mostly sober. She needed to hold herself together for Katrina and Kerry's wedding. She had taken off work to help decorate the sanctuary this afternoon. *Must admit, it looks beautiful. Like Katrina. Guess I know why they always use the word "radiant" to describe the bride.*

Don't know why Katrina picked such odd music, though it was one of Pastor Willard Linger's favorites. Katrina really missed him. We grew up in this church. I only became Methodist because of Travis. Maybe I'll switch back to Presbyterian. Will have to see what the new minister is like.

Okay now. Katrina gave the nod. It was time for her to sing. She'd just do a few bars tonight.

Cressa playing the introduction. Damn! I mean darn. Couldn't remember the words. Glanced over at Cressa. She handed Ingrid the hymnal on the organ console.

Ingrid leafed through it to find "The Lord Ascendeth Up on High." *Still think this is a weird wedding song. Number Two-Twelve. Here it is.*

Something in the way. An index card—looks like Travis's writing on it. But what is…? Getting dizzy. Omigosh…

I saw Ingrid's blue eyes widen as she read something on the card. Her face drained to an ashy white color just before she fell. I reached her first because I was closest; I just had to swivel around and jump off the bench. She was out for less than a minute. Her eyes fluttered, then opened. She tried to sit up, but fell back onto the carpet.

Ingrid's sister Katrina was the next to reach her. She patted Ingrid's face and hovered until Kerry, the groom, gently shouldered her aside and knelt.

"I'm an EMT," he told me. "Let me look at her." He crouched beside her and felt her pulse. "Ingrid, what year is it? Who's the president?"

When she answered, slowly, but correctly, Kerry stood up.

"She'll be okay, but she needs to lie down for a while. And could someone get her some water or juice?"

Kristina ran to the church basement for some grape juice, and the rest of the wedding party milled about. Soon after drinking the juice, Ingrid's color returned and the rehearsal continued. She told me she had a shock seeing one of Travis's index cards. We skipped the singing of the hymn for now.

After I played the recessional and the wedding party had thoroughly practiced filing out, Ingrid rushed back down the central aisle before I could turn the organ off.

"We can practice the piece now if you want," she said.

"Are you sure? We could do it tomorrow before the ceremony if you'd rather."

"No, no. I want to do it now." The hymnal still lay on the floor where she had dropped it and she stooped down to pick it up. She turned to the number and we ran through it. Her fluid voice took the high E flats in stride and made them sound easy. But I shivered inside as I recalled the last time I had played this piece, probably just as Reverend Linger was flinging himself from the church tower. Or maybe he died during the third hymn I played that day—this one was the second.

"I think this is a crazy song for a wedding," said Ingrid.

"I agree. But I've seen much stranger things. A bride wanted *Music of the Night* from 'Phantom of the Opera' just a couple years ago."

"Wow. That's morbid."

She laughed with me as I agreed. It was good to see her back to normal, no ill effects of her fainting episode evident.

I was turned half away, picking up my things, but was able to see her stick the index card, the one that caused her fainting spell, back into the hymnal before she set it on the organ. I picked up my purse and music bag, dawdling while she left the sanctuary so I could take a look at the card. What was written on the back of it almost caused me to swoon too. After I changed shoes I trotted up the aisle and left the church.

Ingrid waved goodbye to me in the parking lot and we parted. She was going to the rehearsal dinner, but I was going to the police station. It had been a long day, but it wasn't over yet.

Chapter 29

Irresoluto: Irresolute, undecided, vacillating (Ital.)

I wasn't prepared for what I saw when I opened Friday morning's paper at my kitchen table, but I should have been. Another find of mine was printed. This one, the text of Willard Linger's suicide note, the one I had found on the back of the index card:

> My dear flock,
> Please forgive me for what I am about to do. It seems the only way. The high places have called me and called me until I can't ignore them any longer. I believe this is the Lord's will. I have done terrible things for which I will now atone. To all the people I have wronged, understand that the defect was always in me, not in you. I will state that an intruder is in the church and I am frightened of him. This will not be true. I am going to my death of my own volition. It is time.

This morning I was in the frame of mind to ponder the words, and to consider exactly what they meant.

Pastor Willard's suicide note had been on the back of the list of hymns he gave to me the day he died, the hymns I played as he flung himself from the bell tower. What an idiot I was! Why hadn't I turned the index card over? Had Ingrid seen it? She must have—why else would she have fainted?

The news article mentioned that Joshua Butardi was still being sought for the murder of Powell Peckham, implying that he was no longer wanted for Reverend Linger's death.

I no longer knew what I believed. It was hard to even tell what I felt. It seemed my whole life was being lived between the notes—I didn't know what key I was supposed to be in, what the chords were, or even where the staff lines were.

Barry did not kill Pastor Willard Linger, but there was still Powell's unsolved murder. Maddy was going to support and believe in Barry, whether or not he had killed Powell. I didn't know if our new friendship could sustain itself if Barry were guilty. I couldn't be honest with her right now. I couldn't admit that it looked to me like Maddy's brother might be a murderer. How could I do that to her?

On top of everything else, I was upset with Daryl. He had no appreciation for the trauma I was going through, and I didn't think I could turn to him for support after our last call. Why did we think we could carry on a long-distance relationship? We hadn't known each other very long—probably not a good foundation for making it through an indefinite separation.

I went through the motions of studying the Bach, but wasn't making any progress. I knew that, in rehearsal, I tended to take some passages at the wrong tempos and realized that I needed to work on the transitions from one movement to the next. When the phone rang, I was uselessly drumming my baton on my kitchen table, keeping time to my pumping knee.

Roger answered my hello.

"Oh, hi, Roger."

"Say, do you need a distraction tonight? I just had a meeting canceled for this evening. I'm pretty sure you've been going through hell lately, discovering bodies right and left."

I had to smile at the way he put it.

"So how about meeting me at Lord Fletcher's?"

He gave me directions and we set a time, late, after the wedding of Ingrid's sister. I set the receiver down and flinched as the phone rang immediately. Naturally, it was Daryl. Our conversation was brief and strained and did nothing to heal our rift. Actually, after I hung up, I wondered if he had even felt my tension.

Neek called just before I left.

"Cressa!" She sounded breathless, which was nothing new, but there was panic in her breathing tonight. "Don't go out. I mean it! You can't do anything tonight. It isn't too late, is it?"

"Too late for what?"

"I mean nothing horrible has happened yet, has it?"

I closed my eyes, seeing Powell's smashed skull, then Willard's broken body. "Neek, horrible things have been happening almost since I got here. You know that."

"But nothing new today, right? Right?"

"Nothing disastrous today. You're right."

She expelled a shaky breath. "I'm panicking here, Cress. This omen was igneous. Straight from the bowels of the earth. This is nothing but a bright neon danger sign."

"You found a neon igneous rock?"

"No! Be serious! This is a dire warning. Don't ignore it."

It was uncanny how often her predictions turned out to be true, but I was pretty sure this one had arrived late. "Okay, Neek. I'll be careful."

I had to go out, though. That couldn't be avoided.

Ingrid resented the intrusion that damned index card had caused. She wanted her sister's wedding to be perfect, to be beautiful.

Hadn't told Katrina anything about it. Even managed to keep her away from the coverage of it in the paper and on TV, thank God. Cressa must have found it after she left.

Now, time to sing to the God with a capital G. Have to make sure little sister's wedding is perfect. Cressa is playing the intro. I wonder what her involvement is in these deaths? People started dying after she came here. Maybe she stirred something up?

No, it must have to do with people who've known Powell longer.

There's my entrance.

Ingrid's voice was on tonight and she felt she sang like the soprano member of the angel choir. One little skipped measure of rest was deftly caught by Cressa. *Have to thank her afterward.*

Katrina's beaming bride's face was all the thanks Ingrid needed as she sat when her number was finished.

Nope, don't think Cressa killed Powell. Arthur, though, he's always had it in for him. Knew Powell a few years ago, from what he says. Sure doesn't like him, though. Hates me, too. Hope he doesn't go after me. Ingrid shuddered.

I got away from the wedding crowd and drove down the highway in the early winter dark, flicking on the dome light at each turn to glance at Roger's directions. After getting off Highway 394, the route was convoluted and the roads were narrow. Finally, I reached the parking lot and walked through a gentle snow flurry into the restaurant.

Roger was waiting right inside the door.

"Is Granddaddy's okay?" he asked.

"I have no idea what you're talking about. You mean Old Grand-Dad?"

He laughed. "No, it's one of the dining rooms."

"Granddaddy's," he said to the hostess and we followed her to a table next to the window.

"This is beautiful," I said, meaning it, too. Beyond a huge wooden patio was Lake Minnetonka. Lights played on the rippling water, and an empty dock stood nearby.

"That's the West Arm Bay." Roger pointed out the window. "In the summer, everyone eats out on the deck. You can pull up in your boat and walk in."

A huge stone fireplace roared and the candles on the table winked. I felt myself relaxing and, maybe, coming around, being present.

"I'm glad it's not too formal," I said. "I've been practicing over at First all afternoon—then there was the wedding today at Heights—and I just came straight from there."

After we ordered a half carafe of chardonnay, I brought up my problem with tempos in the Bach.

"I think I know how each movement should go, but sometimes I start out wrong, then I don't know what to do."

His eyes crinkled in the candlelight as he smiled. I began to wonder how old he was. I knew he was older than me, but didn't know how much.

"Honesty is the best policy," he said. "If it's extremely wrong, just stop, tell them it's your mistake, and start over."

"I'm sure you're right. I guess I don't want to look inexperienced."

"Well, you are, right? And they already know that."

I sighed and took a sip of the wine. It was nice and dry on my tongue. "You're right again."

"On the other hand, if the tempo is just a little off, I keep going until there's an obvious stopping place. Or maybe something that needs correcting right then—someone playing a rhythm or a note wrong. Then I stop, work on the problem, and, when we start over, I suggest we pick up the tempo a little."

"Or slow it down."

"Right, but usually it's the other way for me."

Our server stepped up and took our orders.

The walleye sandwich intrigued me and Roger ordered spaghetti. After an excellent Caesar salad, we dug into our dinners. Without the candle, I couldn't have seen my plate.

"The other problem I have most often is the instruments dragging," he said between bites.

"That's not too bad for me. Sometimes the lower strings lag a little, but generally they stay on my tempo pretty well. Maddy's great at keeping the pace going."

"She is good to work with, isn't she? And how's she doing since all the trouble with her brother?"

"She's frantic. Chamber rehearsal is terrible without her—she really holds the group together."

Roger looked down and shook his head. "What a mess."

"I don't think Barry killed Powell," I announced, startling myself as well as Roger.

He jerked his head up. "Why not?"

I set my sandwich down and started talking with my hands. "It's that note."

"The one they showed on TV?"

"Yes. It was printed in block letters. Barry's handwriting is sloppy and almost unreadable. It's hard to believe that, in the heat of passion—writing an angry note to a lover—he would print neatly."

"Hmm. That would make a flimsy defense, though."

"Oh, I know. But what if someone else left that note where I would be sure to find it? Left it to frame Barry?"

"It's entirely possible. Especially the way you describe it."

"Barry was at Maddy's that night and stayed late, but not late enough to be in the clear."

Roger was tearing at his roll. "I wonder..."

"What?"

"I did a gig with Powell not too long ago. It was a fundraiser for the Red Cross with a luau theme, and they wanted Hawaiian music. Powell sang some Don Ho-type stuff, while I played guitar, and Travis Upton brought his portable keyboard. Powell even played a little ukulele—did you know he played?"

"Travis Upton? The Travis who plays organ at First?"

"The same." He twirled some pasta strands onto his fork, then hesitated bringing the fork up to his mouth. "I thought at the time, well..."

"Thought what?" I asked, chomping a big bite of my sandwich. His hesitation was aggravating me.

"Travis and Powell had driven together over to the gig and, when we were loading up to leave, it looked like—well, it looked like they were *together*."

I blinked. "You said they rode there together…"

"I mean, I came upon them and it looked like they were just pulling apart."

I blinked again. "Oh. Now I see what you mean. You think they were lovers." I paused, thinking furiously. "If they were, and if Barry and Powell were also lovers, then that would mean—"

"You might want to think about how Travis felt, and where he was the night Powell died."

"Yes, I might. Maybe the police should, too."

Thoughts of Powell, Travis, and Barry whirled through my mind the rest of the meal, and I declined dessert, wanting to be alone with my ideas and see where they led. Roger stepped around the little table and held my chair for me. I got up, reached for my purse, and then looked up.

I saw someone duck his head behind a menu as soon as our eyes met. Travis! Sitting alone at the next table. A huge potted fern hid him from Roger, and mostly from me, but in that one glimpse I was sure it was him—and that he was close enough to hear us talking.

I stumbled on my way out, light-headed with dread.

Chapter 30

Pensieroso: Pensive, thoughtful (Ital.)

Roger walked me out to my car and asked if I would like to get dessert somewhere else. "Tomorrow's Saturday," he reminded me as he leaned in close while I scrabbled in my purse for my keys.

"I think I need to go home," I said. "I'm just really tired." *And confused.* I found the keys and pushed the door-open button, then swung in and started the car.

"Okay. But I'd like to see you again." He bent down and I was afraid he was going to try to kiss me, but he gave me a wink instead, then straightened up and leaned on the open door. "Call me anytime if you just want to talk."

"Thanks so much, Roger. I will. I do appreciate all the help you've given me."

At last he closed the door and I drove slowly out of the parking lot, trying to remember how I had come. The way home, of course, was just as complicated as the route to get there, but I managed to find the highway, then my turn-off in Hopkins.

My apartment felt safe tonight. I sat and pushed the remote but, as soon as the television sprang to life, I turned if off.

Powell. Barry. Travis. Could it be?

My face felt hot recalling Travis's stricken eyes at the table next to us in the restaurant. We hadn't noticed him come in, but he had to have been there when we were discussing him. Roger hadn't seen him at all and, to save Travis from further embarrassment, I hadn't mentioned it to Roger. But what an awful thing to overhear! People thinking that you are possibly a murderer.

Okay, but it IS possible.

Travis's words that night haunted me. He had asked Powell, "Who are you with?"

Wasn't that the kind of thing a former lover would ask?

Another phrase stuck, too. Powell saying, "Stupid bitch." Powell was angry at a woman. *Ingrid?* Probably. *Maddy?* Why would he be mad at her?

For that matter, why was Travis eating all alone at Lord Fletcher's? Was he following me?

I rubbed my temples, knowing I wouldn't be able to go to sleep with these thoughts pestering me.

In an effort at distraction, I hauled my new organist bag onto the kitchen table and drew out the sheets of music and the hymnal. Trudy had written down the lectionary verses for me and I had picked out hymns for Sunday. She had to have them from me by Thursday in order to get them into the Sunday bulletin.

I started to open the hymnal to review them, but it was the Methodist hymnal. I must have shoved the wrong one into my bag. The Presbyterian hymnal had to still be at the Methodist choir loft where I practiced this afternoon.

Knowing I probably wouldn't sleep for hours yet anyway, I tugged on my coat and boots and went out to the car to drive over and retrieve my hymnal.

Chapter 31

Brusco: Rough, harsh (Ital.)

Joshua had just about made up his mind to try going home one more time. He ached to rest his head on his mother's shoulder. He remembered sitting next to her when he was little. She read to him every night on the scratchy blue couch. He would lean against her as she soothed him with Dr. Seuss or Shel Silverstein. He knew she would help him. He just needed some help. Just a little help.

It was late, though. He wanted to see his mother, but it wasn't something he wanted to do tonight. Tonight he was cold.

He didn't dare go back to the homeless shelter. The TV said he was wanted and everyone there knew him. Hell, there might even be a reward for turning him in. Those dopers would rat on him in a minute if they got money for it. Someone had probably figured out that Powell was his father. Even so, Josh wouldn't have killed him, for Christ's sake.

The night was bitter and the wind was stiff, as was Joshua's heart. His insides felt dead. He'd been walking for a couple of hours now and needed to get inside somewhere. Last night he had broken a window and stayed inside an empty house that had a "For Sale" sign in the front yard. The heat wasn't on, but it was at least shelter.

He looked up. Where in the hell was he, anyway? Then he recognized the street. Up ahead was a familiar building, the Presbyterian church, the one with that strange old guy.

He started to walk across the dark parking lot to try the front door. He hadn't gone more than a few steps when he saw the cars. Cop cars. He was wanted. They were waiting for him.

Damn, he thought. *I can't get inside even if the old guy forgot to lock up.*

He looked across the busy road to the other one, the Methodist church. It was dark, too, but had lighted lamp posts in the front, illuminating an empty parking lot.

But wait. A car was pulling in. He headed across the street, staying out of the splash of light from the street lamp. As he reached the other side, the stained glass windows lit up dimly. A car stood near the entrance. Not a cop car.

Joshua crept up the stairs and tried the heavy front doors. They swung open and he padded in, debating about whether to try the downstairs room with the couches, or the choir loft with the space heater.

But no, the lights were on in the sanctuary. He'd better head down.

Still, he hesitated. Had he imagined that bloody heap the last time he was here? He stole toward the light, just to take a peek.

He straightened and breathed deep. No, it didn't look like anyone had ever died there. He must have imagined the whole thing. Why was his mind so addled tonight?

There was a puff of breath on the back of his neck, but before he could turn around, strong hands gripped his neck. He struggled to scream, to hit out, but the hands were choking off his voice and his air. Everything went black and silent.

Chapter 32

Chiaro: Clear, pure (Ital.)

I thought I knew what had happened. Travis had practiced at First on Thursday afternoon, and I had been there later in the day because of the wedding preparations at the Presbyterian Church. I could picture the Methodist hymnal lying on the organ bench where Travis had left it. Then, as I practiced the offertory and anthem for Heights, I placed the music beside me as I finished each piece. Travis's Methodist hymnal got shoved into my bag when I left because it was underneath my music.

I didn't plan on practicing again before Sunday morning. I liked to leave a "down" day before a performance. This worship service wasn't truly a performance, but it would be my very first Sunday as the Hopkins Heights Presbyterian Church organist.

I would get to Heights early on Sunday morning, and get both the organ and my fingers warmed up. But tonight I wanted to rehearse the hymns in my head.

I drove past the dark parking lot of Heights and noticed two police squad cars parked beside the adjacent office building—waiting, I presumed, to catch Joshua Butardi. As I turned into First Methodist, I was thankful to see the lights. *Maybe Heights ought to think about getting them, too.*

Since no one else would be there this late on a Friday night, I parked right next to the front steps, in one of the spaces reserved for visitors. It hadn't snowed for several days now, so the pavement was dry, but a sharp wind bit into my face in the short distance between the car and the doors.

Olive had given me my own key so I could come and go as I pleased. She said she could tell I would often keep odd hours. I let myself in and this time, I switched the lights on when I went up the stairs to the choir loft. The last time I went to the choir loft in the dark, I had overheard Powell and Travis below.

I had brought the whole music bag with me and I now set it on the bench. Sure enough, there was my Presbyterian hymnal, sitting open on the organ's music rack. Shaking my head and smiling at my own absentmindedness, I drew Travis's hymnal from the canvas carry-all by its spine. Two index cards fell out and landed beneath the organ pedals.

Damn! Oops, shouldn't say that in church. But damn anyway.

I would have to get down on my hands and knees to retrieve them. I stooped, reached, then froze. One of the cards had landed face up. On it was written a list of hymn numbers and some notes Travis had written to himself. After the first hymn, the note said "third verse *a capella,*" and next to the last hymn was written "last verse—alternate ending."

The notes were printed neatly. In exactly the same way as the note from Barry to Powell. The printing was identical.

Of course. Suddenly everything became clear. It was as if a puzzle made of notes had been whirling in my brain and, in an instant, all the notes fit together like a master composition.

Travis used index cards for his hymn notes. I had seen him sticking them into his hymnal. If Travis had written the note framing Barry, then he had probably killed Powell.

"Travis," I whispered. "It was Travis."

I worked both the cards out from under the pedals and straightened up.

Travis stood facing me with pure, hard hatred in his eyes.

Chapter 33

Hurtig: Swift, headlong (Ger.)

For an endless expanse of time we faced each other, motionless. Travis was breathing audibly, almost panting. I wondered if he had run up the steps—then I wondered if he had followed me here to the church. *Of course!* He *did* hear me talking to Roger about him and Powell's murder at Lord Fletcher's. He followed me to the apartment, then here.

Would he have come after me in my apartment if I hadn't left? Surely I would have been safer there. It seemed I was making it easy for him. An incongruous vision of a bright neon orange igneous rock floated through my swirling consciousness.

A low sound came from his throat. He was growling at me! I looked into his eyes and an animal looked back.

I judged the distance between us to be about ten paces. He stepped forward. Now it was nine.

The heavy black music stand was at the edge of my vision. I still held the index cards, the damning index cards, in my hand. Travis's eyes flicked down to them, then back to my face.

Our eyes locked and I didn't dare look away, afraid he would spring upon me, strangle me and throw me over the railing. Now I knew he had murdered Powell—and he knew that I knew.

It became as clear as an A440 tuning pitch what I needed to do. I stood perfectly still—in spite of the adrenaline surging, zinging through me—readying me to save my life the only way I could.

Travis shuffled another two steps, still gasping for air, making so much noise he didn't hear what I heard—the gentle bump of the front doors falling shut. I lost focus for a moment, listening for footsteps, then he was upon me.

Before I could blink, his fingers were on my throat, pressing. I couldn't utter a sound. I clawed at his hands with my nails, but, although my grip was strong, his was stronger.

Kick! If I can't remove his hands I have to kick him.

I drew my foot back, but before I could bring it forward he swung me around and I lost my balance.

Those iron hands! Air—I need air. Please, air.

Now I was hanging from his deadly grasp. The choir loft was starting to disappear around the edges. I could feel blood pounding in my head, and I was afraid I would pass out. So much for my plan to save my life.

He shook me back and forth like a cat toying with a mouse.

My elbow brushed something metal. We had scooted across the floor. I grabbed behind me and clutched the stem of the music stand, tipped the song sheets off it, hoisted it, and swung the heavy top as hard as I could at his head. It caught him by surprise and he went down, losing his grasp of my throat.

I stood for just a half a second, drawing sweet air through my aching throat, before I leapt over him and hurled myself down the stairs. Halfway down, I crashed into a very solid man rushing up. I let out a tiny sound of delight at his police uniform, flattened myself against the wall, croaked, "He's up there," and watched another nice, solid policeman clatter past me.

Chapter 34

Filo di voce: The very softest and lightest vocal tone (Ital.)

I must have lost consciousness for a minute or so. When I came back to the world, I was being carried by strong arms into the cold night air. My cheek lay against a hard metal button.

"Ed, help me here," said the man carrying me. I opened my eyes as one uniformed policeman handed me to another one, who gently slid me into the passenger seat of his patrol car.

After a couple of minutes, two more uniforms came down the church steps, manhandling Travis, hands cuffed behind him, and pushed him into the other squad car.

"How did—" I started. My sore throat made speech difficult. I swallowed and spoke more softly. "How did you happen to be here? Were you following me?"

"No, we were following *him*." He gestured to the back seat, behind the protective grillwork, where a young, scared, very dirty young man lay across the seat. "We were looking for him to return either here or there." He thumbed toward the Presbyterian church. "We watched this guy go inside, then your friend there followed him. When we got there, this kid here was layin' on the floor. Your guy knocked him out. Me and Officer O'Brien carried him out and the other two over there followed that guy up the stairs. Guess he attacked you, too?"

"He tried to strangle me," I whispered, touching my voice box. "I don't know if I'll ever talk right again." Or sing. I hoped I could sing eventually.

More cars arrived and officials swarmed into the church. At one point, a police officer closed the car door and turned on the heat. At another point, someone brought me my purse and I fished out the key so they could lock up. I heard a discussion that led to the decision not to seal anything off with police tape. Someone thought to ask me who should be told about the happenings that night. I squeaked out Melvin and Olive's names, and fumbled with my phone to bring up their numbers.

I spent the rest of the night in the hospital "under observation." As soon as I was released in the morning, I took a cab to get my car, then drove to a drugstore to get some cough syrup.

Back in my apartment, I swigged the syrup—it felt wonderful trickling down my throat. I took three aspirin and slept for hours.

Chapter 35

Sec: Dry, simple (Fr.)

Joshua, once again, didn't have any idea where he was when he woke up. This time, though, it all came flooding back within seconds. Those hands around his throat, being bundled into the back of the police car, finally his mother at the police station. Her eyes were as red and puffy as on the night his dad had left them.

What he hadn't been prepared for was how he felt when she touched his face. The sensation made him wish he were an infant again so he could crawl into her lap. They had cried in each other's arms until the cop came and pulled them apart.

He didn't like it here, but he knew it was the best place for him right now. This time he was determined to make it through rehab. His mother had promised to take him back. She put conditions on it, but his counselor was on her side. He said the conditions were reasonable. He had to get a job—didn't matter what kind, just a job, and he had to hand over his whole paycheck to her for a year.

Josh would never admit it to anyone, but he was sick of being cold and trying to steal enough to feed his habits. He was going to break all of them here.

He wasn't sure if that minister, Pastor Tucker, was being straight with him. But if he was, Josh had a job for after rehab as a janitor in the Methodist church. Tucker had gotten a stern look on his face when he told Josh that he wouldn't be allowed to sleep in the church. When Joshua grinned at that, the minister grinned back.

Chapter 36

Intimo: Heartfelt, fervent (Ital.)

I had a champagne glass in one hand and the other firmly on Daryl's arm as I said, "Daryl, this is Roger Hirt. He's been a big help to me." I had pictured this introduction many, many times, not sure if it would ever happen.

"Glad to meet you." Roger turned to me. "It went very well."

"How were the tempo changes?" I asked. Those had been my main concern for this concert. The Bach had so many movements, each with a different tempo.

"They were all smooth. The Sarabande started a little slow, but you got it on track. I doubt anyone noticed."

"I didn't," said Daryl. "All the pieces sounded great to me."

That's the thing about concerts. There's never been a perfect one in the history of the world, yet every player and every conductor pick apart every little thing afterward. I guess you can't grow and improve if you don't. But you also can't expect perfection. I'd been told that so many times, someday I might believe it.

Most of the glitches noticed by everyone on stage are lost to the audience, which is a very good thing. The main trick is to act like that's what you meant to do—that's how the piece should be played. They'll go along with you unless you do something so drastic you have to stop and start over.

"Pretty fancy reception." Daryl gestured at the tables, covered in white linen and laden with plates of tiny cakes, fruits, cheeses, and hand-dipped chocolate-covered cherries. "Even if it is in a church basement."

"I haven't talked to you in ages," Roger said as he grabbed a glass of wine from the passing waiter. "Looks like your new church likes you. Enough to host your first concert, anyway."

"It's not really new anymore. I started playing organ for them in January, so I've been here almost two months."

"Terrible business about the minister." Roger shook his head.

"Yes, the congregation is still interviewing new pastor candidates. The fellow we talked to last Sunday gets my vote. Oh, there's Maddy. Excuse us, Roger."

I pulled Daryl across the fellowship hall of the Presbyterian church and introduced them.

"This is the secret of my success," I said to Daryl. "An excellent first chair."

"I'm just glad you worked out," Maddy kidded, a crooked smile on her face and a wink in her eye. "Otherwise it would make me look bad."

She seemed back to normal. I asked if she had heard from Barry.

"He loves it in Chicago. Our baby brother Frank sees him at least once a week. I'm glad Frank got a job there, too, and so close to Barry. He lost the contract he was working on when he was in jail, naturally. Since he had to make a new start, he figured he'd do it with a clean slate."

An older couple, longtime members of Heights, walked up and congratulated Maddy and me on the performance. We both beamed like first graders winning a spelling bee.

I knew I would completely deflate later that night, but for now the glow of my first chamber ensemble concert buoyed me up. Daryl's presence did something for me, too. We continued to be off-and-on in our long-distance relationship, but for tonight, we were right on.

Ginny Dahlberg greeted us after the couple went to check out the tables behind us. I introduced her. "Daryl, this is the director of the Nursery School at the Methodist church."

"Hi, pleased to meet you. Cressa's told me about your illness."

"Next Monday will be my first day back at work full-time." She beamed at the three of us, then turned to Maddy. "And you'll never guess—or maybe you will—who sent me a get-well card."

Maddy tilted her head and shrugged.

"Your brother."

"Barry?"

"Yes. It was a sweet gesture. Tell him I really appreciate it. I'm feeling so good lately, I'm ready to bury any and all hatchets. Tell Barry, no hard feelings, and wish him well for me. Okay?"

Maddy gave Ginny a hug. All was right with the world.

Acknowledgements

I wish to thank my publisher, Barking Rain Press, and my two editors there, Rachel Roddy and Ti Locke, for getting this book polished up and ready for publication.

I owe much to the good people at Hopkins United Methodist Church in Hopkins, Minnesota. I have changed the name of the church, but not the appearance of their beautiful building. None of the people I knew when I was the church secretary there inspired any of the characters. Every person is fiction, bears no resemblance to a living person I've known, and they all came from my imagination. I also changed the name of Faith Presbyterian Church and used its location.

Very early editions were helped by feedback from Michelle Yep-Martin, Cathy Sonnenberg, and Pauline Alldred.

Hope Publishing has kindly given permission for me to use a few of the words from Natalie Sleeth's incredibly moving piece, "Hymn of Promise."

Kaye George

Kaye George

Kaye George is a short story writer and novelist who has been nominated for three Agatha awards. She is the author of several mystery series including the *Imogene Duckworthy* humorous Texas series and the *Fat Cat Mysteries* series. *Eine Kleine Murder,* the first book in the *Cressa Carraway Musical Mystery* series, was a Silver Falchion Finalist. Her short stories can be found in her collection, *A Patchwork of Stories*, as well as in *Fish Tales: The Guppy Anthology*, *All Things Dark and Dastardly*, *Grimm Tales*, and in various online and print magazines. She reviews for *Suspense Magazine,* writes for several newsletters and blogs, and gives workshops on short story writing and promotion. Kaye lives in Knoxville, Tennessee. Find out more at her website, or through Twitter and Facebook.

WWW.KAYEGEORGE.COM

About Barking Rain Press

Did you know that five media conglomerates publish eighty percent of the books in the United States? As the publishing industry continues to contract, opportunities for emerging and mid-career authors are drying up. Who will write the literature of the twenty-first century if just a handful of profit-focused corporations are left to decide who—and what—is worthy of publication?

Barking Rain Press is dedicated to the creation and promotion of thoughtful and imaginative contemporary literature, which we believe is essential to a vital and diverse culture. As a nonprofit organization, Barking Rain Press is an independent publisher that seeks to cultivate relationships with new and mid-career writers over time, to be thorough in the editorial process, and to make the publishing process an experience that will add to an author's development—and ultimately enhance our literary heritage.

In selecting new titles for publication, Barking Rain Press considers authors at all points in their careers. Our goal is to support the development of emerging and mid-career authors—not just single books—as we know from experience that a writer's audience is cultivated over the course of several books.

Support for these efforts comes primarily from the sale of our publications; we also hope to attract grant funding and private donations. Whether you are a reader or a writer, we invite you to take a stand for independent publishing and become more involved with Barking Rain Press. With your support, we can make sure that talented writers thrive, and that their books reach the hands of spirited, curious readers. Find out more at our website.

WWW.BARKINGRAINPRESS.ORG

ALSO FROM BARKING RAIN PRESS

VIEW OUR COMPLETE CATALOG ONLINE:

WWW.BARKINGRAINPRESS.ORG

Manufactured by Amazon.com
Columbia, SC
01 April 2017